Shattered

Hearts

Shattered Hearts

Stacy Lynn Carroll

Dedicated to all the WoPAs out there, especially those who are suffering in silence. You are beautiful! You are strong! You are not alone!

Books by author Stacy Lynn Carroll:

Adult:
My Name is Bryan
Shattered Hearts

Young Adult:
The Princess Sisters
Frogs & Toads
Forever After

Children:
A Tale of Tails
The Yowlers

Chapter One

D ear Sarah,
    I know what you're going through. You feel
    sick, afraid, angry, sad, confused. Your trust
has been completely broken, and you don't know how to get it
back. You're questioning everything. What else did he lie
about? Take a minute: breathe. This is not your fault. Your
husband has an addiction to pornography. It helps to say it
out loud. I understand that right now you are in shock. This
amazing man who you've been married to for fifteen years has
kept his dark secret from you, and from everyone. I'm going to
repeat myself. This is not your fault. Now, looking back, you
can see the warning signs. You wonder how you didn't catch
them before. You will drive yourself mad wondering what if.
You can't go back and do anything to change the past. That's
over. You get to decide your future now. I know you're feeling
overwhelmed with kicking him out and suddenly being
thrown into the role of single mom to your five beautiful
children. Pause your thoughts for a moment and take some
deep breaths. You have support. People love you. You're going
to get through this. One step at a time.

The first step is you need to take care of yourself. You're feeling lower than you have in your entire life. You can't even think about healing your relationship with him unless you heal yourself first. Take the kids to your mom's house today and do something to make you feel good about yourself. Go get a pedicure, get a new haircut, or buy yourself a nice new outfit. You deserve it. You are not worthless. You are loved.

Sincerely, a friend

I reach forward and slam the laptop shut. Shoving my chair back, I stand from my desk, hands trembling. What a stupid, nosy jerk! Who do they think they are, telling me what to do and how to live my life? How did this person even find out? I swipe at the never-ending stream of tears and walk across the hall to the bathroom. I flip on the cold water and splash some on my face. I look up into the mirror as I reach for the faded blue hand towel and dry my flushed cheeks. I am ugly. My eyes are so swollen and red, I look like the victim of an angry bee attack.

I am a victim.

I was happy. I was fine. We were perfect together—everyone says so. We built this life together. For fifteen years, we've worked hard and sacrificed to provide for our children. My mind wants to scream a thousand profanities at my husband for being too willing to throw away everything we ever wanted for a few seconds of . . . I don't even want to think about it. My mouth falls open to scream the pain I feel, but I stop myself in case one of the kids is awake. My red, splotchy skin is not the result of an insect, but I was stung bad, and by the person who promised to always have my back and walk by my side.

I can hear the twins talking in their room, and I know my solace will soon be over. I can't let the kids see me like this. I have to be strong for them. I reach out and click the lock on the bathroom door before turning on the shower and stepping in. I allow the hurt and the anger to run down my face alongside the hot water. My body is numb. Steam pours out of the faucet as I make the water hotter, just to feel something. I lean forward and rest my head against the bitter cold tile. The cold sends shivers down my spine, despite the scalding water against my back. My legs buckle, and I collapse to the floor of the tub. Pulling my knees up to my chest, I rest my head on them and sob. My body begins to convulse and the sourness building in my stomach gives way. The warm, putrid smell of vomit floats up to my nostrils. I reach for the soap dish and pull myself upright again.

I can hear the kids fighting in the hallway, which means they are all awake. How am I going to do this? How am I going to raise five kids all by myself? My breathing grows ragged as the sobs continue to wrack my body. The kids are going to want to know where daddy is. What do I tell them? I turn in the shower and look up so the stream of burning water washes down my face. I continue to stand there, despite the pounding against the bathroom door. I can barely hear it over the screaming worry that's now consuming my mind. I wash my body again and again, but no matter how much I scrub, I still feel disgusting. My skin stings, red and raw. It's amazing how seeing just one repulsive image can make me feel completely worthless.

"I'll be right back," I say to the kids, sliding the van door closed and rushing back into the house. I know Daniel says he has too much work to do, but I hate going to another family party without him. My hurrying feet take me down the basement steps. Maybe I can convince him to meet us there, if he finishes early. I approach his office door and am surprised to find it open a crack. He usually locks it. Daniel seems to be shut away there so often now.

I push the door open. My mouth opens, but whatever I was about to say is forgotten. I take in the image of a blonde on the computer screen and stare in confused disbelief as her bikini top falls to the floor. My head begins shaking in denial that Daniel would be looking at something like this. The light from the screen falls with a blue whisper of enticement on my husband's lips, which are opened in hunger, his eyes lit with lust. I squeeze my eyes shut, but the image remains, permanently ingrained in my mind. I reach for the door and stumble into it with a loud THUD.

Daniel jumps from his seat, almost tripping as he zips up his pants. I can't bear to look at him as his fingers clumsily struggle to hide his depravity. He's like a boy caught with his hand in the cookie jar, but in this case, his hand is caught with something much more vile.

Neither one of us speaks. The oxygen has been sucked from the room, the invisible vacuum taking my soul with it. I struggle on the inhale of a shaky breath as my face falls and with it my tears. Daniel's face blurs in front of me, obscuring the man I thought I knew. I crumple to the ground. I can't stand. I can't breathe. I can't look at him.

The man who promised to love me forever, who touched my cheek sweetly when he kissed me, the man who held my babies with such gentleness and awe, the man who played catch with my son and teared up with pride at my daughter's dance recital, that man was gone. This beautiful image has been ripped away from me with his betrayal.

"Sarah, I'm..." He can't even finish it. He knows it isn't enough.

"How could you do this to me?" I whimper. "How can I not be enough for you?"

Daniel moves down onto his knees before me as if to comfort me. I never give him the chance.

"Don't touch me!" I scream, shoving him away. My tears become hot with anger. I don't want to stay in this room, the promiscuous girl on the screen mocking me. My shaky legs struggle into a standing position.

"How could you?" I manage, my voice breaking along with my heart.

He stands across from me and shakes his head in shame. "I don't know." He reaches out for me, but I take a step back, shaking my head.

"Don't even come near me. You promised. You even swore to me on my father's grave that you were done with all..." My hand signals toward the repulsive girl, my mind searching for the right word to describe it all. "That," I hiss. His hands go into his hair, his face flushing red with shame and revulsion.

"I don't know what's wrong with me." His fingers
pull at his hair, almost hysterical at his own vile actions. His
eyes begin to water as he stares at me for help.

"You're sick," I say, retreating into the hallway. *"You
need to get some professional help."* I turn to go.

"Sarah, please," he begins to beg.

"Get out," I say, my voice low and threatening. *"I'm
taking the kids to your nephew's birthday party. I want you
gone before we get back."*

"Sarah, wait." He grabs at my hands, my clothes, my
feet, desperately pleading for one more chance.

"No, Daniel, I've waited long enough." My voice is ice
cold. *"If you aren't gone, I will call the police to remove you.
Now get out of my house and don't come back."*

I want to forget last night. I want to wake up from
this nightmare and have my life back again. As the
banging and screaming continue to grow louder, I know
the nightmare is now my reality. I finally slam the
handle down. I can't hide anymore. I take deep breaths
and try to think of the good while I quickly run the small
towel over my body. My beautiful children are the good
in my life. No matter what happens, I have them forever.
He stole everything from me. My heart, my soul, my
dignity, but he will never be able to steal my love for
them. I throw my sweats back on and step into the
chaos.

My little two-year-old, my baby, is sobbing
uncontrollably about needing his morning orange juice.
He grabs at my legs, pulling my sweatpants partway

down as he tries to scale my body. "Mommy! Mommy, orange juice!" he cries.

I turn to my beautiful eleven-year-old, my eyes pleading for help. "Olivia, would you get your brother some orange juice, please?"

"I tried, Mom, he just screamed at me and threw it across the room. He wants Mommy's orange juice."

I sigh deeply and scoop the bawling child into one hand while readjusting my waistband with the other. Once he's situated on my hip, I turn to the twins who have been arguing since I made an appearance.

"I'm hungry!"

"I want cereal."

"Well, I want cinnamon cereal."

"I get the pink bowl!"

"I wanted the pink bowl!"

"No fair, you had it last time."

"No, you did!"

"I did not, you liar!"

I step between them just as Maddy lunges at Addy. Balancing Jaxon on my other hip, I crouch down so their five-year-old eyes are level with my own. "You have two choices," I say, holding up my fingers. "You can choose to stop fighting, go downstairs, and have some breakfast. Or you can stay up here and fight and remain hungry. It's up to you." I reach out and grab the wall behind me, leaning on it for support as I stand again. The twins stare at each other before racing away.

"I bet I can run downstairs faster than you."

"Nu-uh, I'm the fastest!"

Olivia rolls her eyes and walks slowly toward the staircase. "Where's Dad, Mom? Did he go to work early this morning?"

I freeze in my tracks. I still don't know what to tell them. I can feel the lump I've been battling with all morning start to rise in my throat again, preparing to attack. I carefully avoid Olivia's eyes while I walk down the stairs toward the kitchen. "Daddy has a few projects he needs to work on. He might be gone for a little while." There. Simple. Not too many details, and not a complete lie either. I smile at her weakly, hoping she'll drop the subject. She doesn't seem quite satisfied with my answer, but she doesn't question anything else. "Where's Danny?" I ask, looking around the messy kitchen. I walk straight over to the refrigerator and pull on the sticky handle, mentally adding it to the list of things needing to be cleaned, and pull out Jaxon's sippy cup of orange juice. Placing it in his hands, I'm finally able to put him down. He runs over to the crayon-streaked table and climbs up into his booster seat.

"I think Danny is still sleeping," Olivia says.

I stare past her, thinking of all the times I thought my husband was still sleeping beside me in bed, when he was actually...

"Jaxon wants bagel." My thoughts are interrupted by my son's cute toddler voice.

"How does Jaxon ask?"

"Pwease."

"No fair! We were here first!" Addy yells.

"Yeah, where's my cereal?" Maddy adds.

Suddenly filled with worry about what my nine-year-old might be doing, I dash back upstairs. I can hear 'mom' being yelled by several voices behind me but my legs move forward anyway. I throw open his door in a panic. He's still asleep in bed, just like Olivia said. I try and shake the anxiety from my mind and racing heart as I walk back downstairs. What is wrong with me? I'm terrified of sleeping now?

When I walk in, I see the twins have pushed stools over to the counter and are pouring cereal into their bowls. Cereal drops all over the floor and Jaxon is stomping each fallen piece into dust. Olivia is trying to stop them all, but they're ignoring her and giggling. I rush forward just as Maddy tips the full gallon of milk over her bowl. The white liquid rushes over her cereal, the force of the flow pushing her breakfast off the edge of the counter and all over the ground. Jaxon squeals and begins jumping with both feet in the puddles of mushy mess. I grab the now half empty gallon from Maddy's hands and put it away. She begins to holler and cry over her lost breakfast. Addy climbs down from her stool and joins Jaxon on the floor. The two of them giggle with pleasure as they squish the now-soggy cereal between their toes.

I scoop up Maddy and tell her we can make more. Then I move over to the sink and rinse a rag. I begin mopping up the milk, which is running down all sides of the countertop like a giant waterfall. Olivia's sensitive nose gets the better of her and she begins dry heaving over the smell of warm dairy. I send her from the room and try desperately to keep the kids out of the mess while I clean up the counter and floor. Maddy continues to pull on my arm, whining for me to get her new food right now. My mind flashes back to that email this morning. I can't give in and go to my mom for help. I'm strong enough to handle this on my own. Besides, if I follow the e-mail, I'll just prove they were right. I hear a loud crash upstairs followed by Danny's voice. "I didn't do it." I scrunch my mouth and squeeze my eyes shut.

"Do you guys want to go to Grandma's today?"

Chapter Two

I stare at the fashion magazine resting on my lap. The woman on the cover is a blur through my tears. The buzzing of hair dryers and snipping of scissors echo throughout the small salon. My nostrils burn with the smell of perm solution from the lady at my right. Why am I here? If I change my appearance to look more like one of these models, isn't that becoming an object for him to lust after? I brush the magazine off like a bug, and it crashes to the floor. I close my eyes and lean back in the uncomfortable plastic chair.

Daniel brushes a strand of long, auburn hair from my face. He twirls the lock between his fingers.

"I wonder what you would look like as a blonde," he says. "Have you ever considered dyeing your hair?"

I roll off the bed and reach for my clothes, pulling them on quickly. I can't believe his first thoughts, after the intimate moment we just shared are about changing my appearance. I sniffle.

"What's wrong, Sarah?" he says, almost angrily.

I whip around to face him. "I thought you liked my red hair."

"Geeze, don't be so dramatic. I was just wondering what you would look like. That doesn't mean I don't like the way you look now. I love how long your hair is." He steps from the bed and fondles a strand again before pulling me into his bare chest. "Don't ever cut it," he says, kissing the top of my head.

I remember the image from last night. The blonde. My face burns with a mixture of anger and embarrassment. I'm doing this for me. I'm here because, right now, I need a reason to feel good about myself. Reluctantly, I bend down and scoop the crinkled mass off the floor. I flip through the pages, but there are too many pictures of half-naked women, tanned and perfect in their silk panties and bikini tops. I begin to hyperventilate. I toss the magazine onto an end table and try to calm my ragged breaths.

I pull out my cell phone instead. I notice a red bubble over my e-mail icon and realize a new message awaits. Who would send me an e-mail on a Thursday afternoon? I open the icon and immediately recognize the e-mail address. What in the world? Two in one day? Against my better judgment, I open the message and begin to read.

Dear Sarah,

Confide in a trusted friend. You need to talk to someone. You need a person who will not judge your husband harshly should you reconcile. Keeping these emotions bottled up will only cause the pain to linger. Don't do this alone. So many people in your life love you. Reach out to one of them. Let them help you as you travel down the unknown path which lies ahead.

Sincerely, a friend

The words are exactly what I need to hear and exactly what I don't want to hear. I'm not known for my ability to accept help. When I called my mom and asked if she could watch the kids for a few hours, I thought she was going to die of shock. I never ask for help when I'm capable of doing something on my own. And now this "friend" wants me to share my greatest trial in the entire world with another person. Not only share my secret, but ask for help with it. Who can I even trust with this?

My name is called three times before I register the hairdresser is talking to me. "I'm sorry, my brain is a bit frazzled today," I reply and follow her to the black chair waiting for me.

"No worries, hon, we all have bad days. You wanna talk about it?" She drapes the cape over my head and cinches the snap around my neck.

"No, thanks." I show the woman what I want done, courtesy of a Google image. Then I close my eyes and let her work her magic. Perhaps for the first time in my life, I don't hold a conversation with the hairdresser. She tries to ask me a couple questions, but I only grunt a response. She gives up quickly and focuses solely on snipping away my split ends. If only she could snip away my insecurities along with them.

I watch as the long red tendrils float down to the floor. My husband loves my long hair. It's one of my best features. I grin wickedly when I think of what his reaction will be. I'm not really cutting my hair to spite him. Well, not completely. No, I'm doing this because I'm tired of pleasing everyone. I'm feeling lower than I ever have and for once in my life, I'm going to do something for me.

My phone beeps in my purse and I jump forward.

"Whoa! Don't move unless you want a much shorter hairdo."

"Sorry," I mumble. I feel stupid. I'm just not used to someone else having my kids. What if the text was from my mom and she needs me? Maybe Danny broke his arm, or maybe the twins burned down the house. I can feel the panic starting to rise in the back of my throat again. My face burns and it becomes harder to breathe. I close my eyes and try to think reasonably. My mom ran a daycare out of her home when I was growing up. She has taken care of hundreds of kids. She knows what she's doing. No one is going to die while I get my haircut.

"All done." The hairdresser whips me around to face the mirror and pulls the cover from around my neck. I glance from side to side. I hardly recognize the woman staring back at me. The short bob is something

I've always wanted to try, but was never brave enough to attempt. I suddenly feel like crying.

"I love it," I choke out. Embarrassed by my sudden emotions, I pay quickly and leave.

Stepping into the bright sun, I squint down at my phone and see the text is from my best friend, Breanna. It's probably been a month since Bre and I last spoke. Some best friend I am. Before I can chicken out, I call her number and put the receiver to my ear.

"Sarah?"

"Hi, Bre."

"Wow, you never call me!"

"I know. I'm sorry, but I always feel like the moment I get on the phone, all five of my children desperately need me."

Breanna laughs. "Oh, I know. Talking to you on the phone is like talking to a person with Tourette's." Breanna laughs at our inside joke. I manage a sad smile. I reach up and touch my mouth. When was the last time I laughed? "To what do I owe this honor?" she asks. "I don't hear screaming in the background, and you haven't cut me off once. Where are the kiddos?"

"They're with my mom."

"Really?"

"Yes, really. I'm taking a me day."

"Wow." I can hear the shock in Breanna's voice. "Good for you!"

"So what are you up to right now? Want to grab some lunch?"

"Seriously?"

"Yeah, are you busy at work?"

"Girl, I haven't had a quiet lunch with you in ages! Even if I had a meeting with the president of the company today, I'd blow it off for some girl time with my BFF."

"You're the best, Bre."

"That's what they tell me."

I smile. Can I really go through with this? "Where do you want to go?" I ask.

"Let's meet at Katy's. It's close to work and I'm dying for a good pastry."

"All right, I'll see you there in half an hour."

"Deal."

"Bye, Breanna."

"Bye, love."

I sit nervously waiting for Breanna. My eyes dart from a happy couple to a group of ladies laughing to the business people sitting across the restaurant. I feel like everyone is watching me. It's like they all know and are silently judging. Before my thoughts can get too grim, Breanna walks in. Her jaw drops at the sight of me. I reach up and self-consciously stroke what remains of my auburn locks.

"Oh my gosh, your hair! I love it! What did Daniel say?"

I freeze. I want to tell her. I need to talk to someone before my brain explodes. But what will she think of me? What will she think of him? Breanna,

Daniel, and I have all known each other since junior high school. The last thing I want to do is damage their friendship or change the way she sees him. I take a deep breath and meet her gaze. Her beautiful brown eyes are filling with worry as they stare into mine.

"Sarah, what's wrong?"

My eyes begin to fill with tears. I stare up at the ceiling, hoping gravity will force them back in. It doesn't work. I blow out a deep breath and decide to go for it. If I can't confide in Breanna, then who can I share this with?

"Daniel and I are separated right now."

"What?" Breanna can't hide the shock on her face. "You two are like the dream team. I've never met a more perfect couple!" She sees the hurt I'm trying to hide and tries to take back her words. "I'm sorry, that probably doesn't help right now." She leans forward. "What happened?"

"Daniel is addicted to pornography." It's the first time I've said the words out loud. Even as they roll off my tongue, I can hardly believe they're true.

"No!" Breanna covers her mouth as several other customers look our way. She reaches out a hand and places it on top of my own. "Oh, sweetie, I'm so sorry! I can't even believe it." She shakes her head. Breanna almost knows Daniel as well as I do. The shock on her face reflects my own. "What happened? How did you find out?"

My mind flashes back to last night. I've relived the memory so many times now, it's burned into me forever. I take a deep breath, and then another. Breanna's face begins to swirl when I can no longer keep back the pooling tears.

"Last night we were supposed to go to his nephew's birthday party. Daniel bailed, telling me he had too much work to do. He's been doing this more and more lately. I find myself a single mom more often than not because he has work or homework or a headache. There's always an excuse with him. Anyway, he helped me load the kids into the van and then we kissed goodbye. Before I even backed out, I realized I forgot to tell him something. I ran back inside and downstairs to his office. I walked in and… and… "

I can't get the words past my lips. I can't describe what it was like to see that yellow bikini fall to the ground and the absolute lust which consumed my husband's eyes. That stupid yellow bikini. It's all I see every time I try to close my eyes. No wonder I can't sleep.

My mouth opens and closes as I try to speak, but the words become tangled in my throat. The tears flow freely now. I'm sure from all the looks I keep getting that my eyes are puffy and my forehead is speckled with red splotches.

"I'm sorry," I whisper. "I'm such a wreck!"

Breanna scoots her chair around to the other side of the table and wraps me in her arms. "I'm so sorry," she whispers. "I'm so sorry you had to walk in on that. I'm so sorry you're going through this. I wouldn't wish this kind of pain on my worst enemy."

Breanna holds me for several minutes while I cry into her shoulder, completely soaking her blue button-up blouse. Our poor waitress comes over to take our order, takes one look at me, and backs away slowly. I don't even have the strength to tell her to stay. I can't remember the last time I ate. I know my body needs food, even though I don't really feel hungry.

"Was last night a complete shock to you then? Did you have any idea this was going on?" Breanna smooths my hair with her hand as I sit upright again and wipe futilely at the mascara waterfall trailing down my cheeks.

"He told me when we were dating that he had struggled with porn as a teen. In my twitterpated state I didn't think to ask questions. I figured it was just in his past. Something a lot of stupid teen boys get mixed up with, but that he was done with that garbage. I mean, why would he continue when he had me, a real woman, now?" I shake my head. "I'm so stupid."

"Hey, don't start that! You are not stupid."

"I caught him one other time, shortly after Danny was born. I found a picture on his computer. He promised me it was a moment of weakness and that he would stop. He even swore to me on my father's grave that he would never look at pornography again. We don't talk about it much. I thought that was the end of it. He promised me, and that was enough. What really gets me is I've asked him a few times over the years if he was still clean and he has always sworn to me that the last time was his last time. If he lied about that, what else isn't he telling me?"

Breanna takes a deep breath and looks me straight in the face. "You need to be strong for the kids. You can't crumple and fall apart. What you need to do now is learn about this addiction. You need the facts or you'll drive yourself crazy with all the 'what ifs,' and especially with the betrayal."

Our waitress begins to tiptoe back in our direction. I plaster a smile on my face, hoping I don't scare her off again. As I watch Breanna order, my mind races back through her words. "I wouldn't wish this on my worst enemy" and "you need to learn about this addiction." Wait. How does Breanna know so much? I place my order without even looking at the waitress. She already thinks I'm a freak anyway. I stare hard at my best friend.

"What?" she asks as soon as the waitress leaves.

"How do you know so much? It's like you've been through this before."

Breanna takes a sip of her ice water and nods. "Did you even wonder why Joe and I split?"

My eyes widen. "You and Joe? Really?"

Breanna reluctantly nods.

"Why didn't you ever tell me? I'm your best friend!"

"All the same reasons you didn't want to tell me today. Shame, embarrassment, afraid of being judged…" Breanna trails off.

I can't believe it. Breanna and Joe have been divorced now for almost two years and I never knew why.

Chapter Three

*D*ear Sarah,
    Talk to your husband. As hard as it is, you need to have a frank discussion with him. You need to know what he is thinking and feeling. You both need to decide if this is something you are going to work through. If it helps, have a friend or a therapist mediate.
    Sincerely, a friend

I am starting to hate this "friend" more and more! What kind of friend won't even tell me who they are? And how on earth do they know what's going on? I toss my phone onto the couch and run my fingers through my short hair.

"I don't want to talk to my husband, thank you very much, and I don't appreciate you telling me to consider his feelings. I don't give a…" I look down at the coffee table where the twins are busy coloring and swallow back the curse words. "Frankly, I don't care what he is feeling right now. He's completely turned my life upside down and made me question the last fifteen years together. Was everything a lie? Why should I care what he thinks or feels?"

Maddy's auburn hair bobs as she looks up at me with her piercing blue eyes. "Mommy, who are you talking to?"

I force a smile. "No one, baby, I'm sorry. I'm just thinking through some things out loud."

"Okay." Thankfully she returns to her coloring book without more questions and I resume pacing our small family room. This time I keep my thoughts internal.

I can hear Jaxon crying upstairs. My body moves slowly, my feet like lead as I pound up each step. I reach the top and have to catch my breath. This is ridiculous! I've never been winded by going up a flight of stairs before. My body can't take much more of this. I need to figure out a way to sleep. Jaxon's crying grows louder, so I pick up the pace and push open his door.

"Hi, baby! Did you have a good nap?"

He rubs his eyes and sniffles. "Daddy?" Every time one of the kids asks for him, it's like a stab to the heart.

"He's not home sweetie, sorry."

Jaxon looks up at me with his round, hazel eyes and I watch helplessly as they fill with tears. I can't take this anymore. I scoop him into my arms and try to soothe his cries while I speed-dial my husband. He picks up on the second ring.

"Hello?"

"Your kids need you."

"I didn't know if I was allowed to call." His voice is low, barely above a whisper, while mine continues to rise.

"Just because I don't want to see or talk to you, doesn't mean our kids understand why their dad is suddenly MIA. It's not easy taking care of them all by myself, you know!"

"You're the one who asked me to leave. I begged you to let me stay. This was your choice." His words are biting.

My cheeks flush with anger. "My choice? You think walking in on my husband jerking off to another woman was MY CHOICE? You actually think I CHOSE to be married to an addict? You think I like where we are right now? Do you think I'm happy that I have to take care of the kids alone and then go to bed by myself every night? No. None of this was my choice. YOU STOLE ALL MY CHOICES FROM ME WHEN YOU CHOSE PORN OVER OUR FAMILY!"

Jaxon whimpers in my arms. I realize I'm still holding him and try to calm my heaving chest and racing heart. I'm so mad right now, my hands are shaking. "Shhhhh, it's okay." I begin rocking back and forth, not sure if I'm soothing Jaxon or myself.

My husband's voice cracks through the phone. "I'm so sorry. I never meant to do this to our family. I never wanted to hurt you." His deep voice trembles as he speaks.

"Well, you did. Now call your kids." *CLICK.*

Hanging up on him might not have been the most mature solution, but it felt pretty great.

Five minutes later my phone rings. I look at it and see my husband trying to video call.

"Kids, your dad is on the phone!" I yell down the hall before I answer and hand the phone to Jaxon. I scoot to the other side of the couch so I don't have to look at Daniel's face.

Jaxon squeals. "Daddy!"

"Hey, buddy."

"Daddy come home?"

"Sorry, buddy, Daddy is really sick right now. I need to get better before I can come home."

"Jaxon kiss better."

"I would love that, Jax." I can hear his voice crack. He pauses before continuing. "But I don't think kisses will make it better this time."

Maddy jumps up from her coloring when Addy comes tearing into the room and they race to the phone. Olivia comes down the stairs close behind them. She stands in the corner of the room, her back against the wall, her arms folded. Addy rips the phone from her brother's hand. He screams in protest and tries to take it back, but she holds the phone just out of reach.

"Hi, Daddy! I miss you. When are you coming home?"

"I'm not sure, Princess. Daddy needs to get better first."

"It's my turn!" Maddy yells, taking the phone from her sister. "I love you, Daddy!"

"I love you too, baby!"

"Give that back!" Addy yells. "I had it first! No fair!"

I grab the phone from the girls, making sure to hold the screen so it's facing out. Jaxon scratches at my legs with his sharp little fingernails, trying to take it back as well. "You all need to be nice and take turns," I say, handing the phone to Olivia. She shakes her head.

"Don't you want to say hi?" I mouth.

Olivia rolls her eyes and shrugs. "Fine, I guess." She takes the phone and says a quick hi before handing it to Addy and walking back upstairs.

Addy accepts it graciously and waves to her father. The other two crowd around her on the couch, both trying to get a glimpse of Daddy while she speaks. I turn and head up the stairs, straight for Danny's room. "Your dad is on the phone downstairs if you want to say hi," I explain after tapping on his door.

Danny looks up from his latest fantasy novel and shrugs. "I'm fine." He goes back to his reading.

"Don't you want to say hi?" I ask. "You haven't seen him in a couple days."

Danny's eyes linger on the final sentence of his chapter. "How is that any different than every other day?"

I close Danny's door and return downstairs, my heart sinking. My husband used to be so good with kids. It's one of the things that first attracted me to him. I knew I always wanted a big family, so when Daniel and I met, he seemed too good to be true. Now as I step back into the living room, I can't even look at his image on the phone. I'm really struggling to remember all the things I loved about him when all I can see right now are the bad. What happened to us?

I know our relationship didn't disintegrate overnight. The last several days apart have given me a lot of time to think. I've pondered all the signs I should have seen but somehow missed. Now they stare me in the face every night, laughing and mocking me while I attempt to fall asleep. His self-esteem has dropped significantly over the years, along with that were increased signs of depression. He stopped wanting to go out and be with other people—friends, family, even his own wife and kids. I should have known as he continued to withdraw from social situations that something deeper was going on. Daniel is super outgoing, an extrovert to a T. So when he started making excuses to stay home, it should have been my first clue something wasn't right.

Daniel has also been quicker to anger lately. My once patient, kind husband is losing his temper, yelling and screaming at the kids at the drop of a hat. This is not the man I married. So why did it take his moving out to actually recognize all these signs?

I felt like my marriage was falling apart for so long, but I could never put a finger on what was actually wrong. I feel so dumb for not figuring it out sooner. Our frequent arguments, his distance and impatience, even his failures at school and work. Everything suddenly makes sense.

I look up when the kids all burst into laughter. That's such a nice sound. Then the kids moan when I hear Daniel say, "Sorry, guys, I gotta go now. I love you all, and tell Mommy I love her too, okay?"

"Bye, Daddy."

"When are you coming home?"

"As soon as I'm all better. And as soon as Mommy says it's okay."

My cheeks flush with anger. How dare he put any of this on me! I try hard not to scoff at his words. Is it possible for him to get "all better?" How would I even know when he is? After all, he lied to me for fifteen years. What's going to prevent him from just lying again?

I rub my temples slowly. All these questions, all these doubts, all this anger are completely exhausting. I feel like I've had a headache for four days straight. After saying goodbye, the kids begin chasing each other and screaming again. I'm not sure how much more my throbbing temples can take. I finally lose it. "QUIET!" The shout that escapes from my throat is so loud, it even startles me. All three of them freeze mid-run. "Upstairs. Pajamas. Now," I say through gritted teeth. Olivia appears and takes a twin by each hand, guiding them up the stairs. Jaxon clambers over to me and demands to be lifted up.

"How do you ask?"

"Pwease."

I scoop him into my arms and carry him up the stairs. My throat is sore from screaming so loud. I shouldn't have done that. My heart aches with guilt. I'm the only parent they have right now. They're confused about what's going on. The last thing they need is to be yelled at more. I bend over the changing table and remove Jaxon's dirty diaper. His eyes are solemn, his face stoic. "Mommy sad?"

I can feel the tears pushing against my eyes, threatening to burst out. "Yes, baby, Mommy is sad."

"Why?"

I'm not sure how to answer, so I sum things up as simply as I can. "I miss Daddy."

Jaxon reaches his little arms out and wraps them around my neck, pulling my face against his warm, bare chest. "It's okay, Mommy."

I smile and kiss his cheek. "Thank you, baby."

"I'm not baby. I'm big boy." His lip juts out in defiance.

"You're right. Thank you, Jaxon." I scoop him up and spin around in a tight hug. He giggles so I spin again. This time it makes my head throb, so I have to sit down.

"Again!"

"I can't, sweetie."

"Again!"

"Jax, I'm just too dizzy."

Maddy tiptoes into the room, her pink princess nightgown swishing against her ankles. "Mommy, can we have stories?"

"Yes, Princess, go pick a book and meet me on my bed."

She squeals and dashes from the room. "I told you Mom's not too tired, Addy. She said yes!"

My shoulders slump when I hear those words. Even my kids know how exhausted I am. I've really been trying to hide it from them. I guess I haven't been doing a very good job. I shift Jaxon to my other hip and carry him into my room, across the hall. We snuggle under the covers and fluff the pillows behind our heads. Addy and Maddy come bounding into the room and climb up onto the bed, each with a book in hand. They slip under the covers on either side of me. Olivia stands in the open doorway, watching.

"Do you want to join us?" I ask.

"I know how to read by myself."

"I know, but that doesn't make being read to any less fun," I say with a smile.

Olivia shrugs and sits at the foot of the bed, pulling the bottom of my comforter over her curled legs. Danny walks past, waving goodnight on his way to his room.

"Danny, wait. Do you want to join us?" I ask.

He just laughs and shakes his head. Apparently that's a no. "Boys are silly," I whisper.

"Girls silly," Jaxon retorts.

I kiss him on the top of his blond little head and begin reading the first book. Halfway through the second, I begin to doze off.

"Mom!"

I jump awake. "Sorry, guys, I guess I'm more tired than I thought."

Olivia reaches across the bed. "Here, Mom, I'll finish."

I smile gratefully and listen to the end of the story. I have to try hard to keep my crazy emotions in check. My 11-year-old is a better mom than I am. I have got to find a way to get sleep! Maybe I really do need to talk to him. If nothing else, maybe I can get some questions answered. At least the ones that are keeping me awake every night.

Once the kids are all tucked into bed, I reach for my cell with shaky hands. I can't even look at his picture on my phone. I push the call button and close my eyes. My heart is pounding and my palms so sweaty, I'm afraid I'll drop the phone. My face flushes when I hear his voice.

"Hello?"

It's the most familiar voice in the world to me, and yet it sounds so foreign now. I'm not even sure what to say, where to start. I should have made notes before calling.

"Sarah? Is everything okay?"

"Hi, Daniel." I release a huge breath of air. "We need to talk."

"Are the kids okay?"

"Yeah, they're fine. Thank you for calling them. You made their whole night."

"Why didn't Danny want to talk?"

"I don't know. I gave him the choice."

"What are you saying to them?" Daniel asks, his voice accusing.

"I'm not saying anything other than you're sick and need to get better before you come home. Don't you dare accuse me of sabotaging your relationship with our kids! You did that just fine yourself." My headache comes back full force. I rest my forehead in my hand and set the phone on my legs. My jaw clenches and unclenches as I wait for his reply. I hate fighting. We're not getting anywhere.

"I still love them," he says quietly. I lift the phone back to my ear. "I still love you." His voice is low and gravelly.

"I need to know what we're doing," I say, ignoring his use of the 'L' word. There's no way I'm ready to respond to a statement like that. "Do you want to stay married?"

"More than anything," he whispers.

"Then what are you doing to fix this? When I asked you to leave, I told you that you needed help."

Daniel clears his throat. "I've been doing a lot of research," he says. "For years, far too many, I thought this was just a bad habit. Something I could stop on my own if I just put my mind to it."

I roll my eyes.

"I learned I was wrong."

My ears prick. Did he really just admit that?

"Pornography is an addiction and it's not something I can just 'get over' on my own. You were right. I need some serious help. I need to see a sex addiction therapist. I've already contacted one and I have an appointment tomorrow."

"Good for you." I really mean it.

"Will you… I mean… would you come with me? Please, Sarah, I'm scared. I don't want to do this alone." Daniel's voice is shaking as he speaks.

"Yes." I say the word before I can give myself an excuse not to go. "What time?"

"It's at 5:30, right after work. Do you want me to see if my sister can watch the kids?"

"Is that where you're staying?"

"Yeah, the first night I slept under my desk at work. I didn't know where else to go. Since then, she's been letting me crash on her couch."

"Sure. I'll drop off the kids at 5:15 and be there to pick you up."

"Thank you, Sarah. I love you"

"Mm-hmm. So does she know?"

"Yes."

"Everything?"

"She knows everything. I had to tell her, since I'm not sure how long I'll be here."

I'm not sure if he's being sincere or just trying to show off his good behavior. I guess I'll find out tomorrow. "And what does she think?"

"She thinks I'm an idiot," Daniel says.

"Well, good. That makes two of us."

My phone beeps, indicating I'm receiving another call. I pull it away from my ear long enough to see my mother-in-law is calling. "Hang on a sec, your mom is on the other line."

"Hello?" My voice is weary.

"Sarah?"

"Hi, Marge, how are you?"

She huffs into the phone. "I cannot believe the way you are treating my son! How do you think I am when I find out my daughter-in-law is trying to break apart a perfectly good marriage and destroy my grandchildren's lives? Shame on you!"

The phone slips through my fingers and drops onto my lap. My cheeks begin to burn with the anger building up behind them. "Excuse me?" I say, picking up my cell again.

"You are making an absolute big deal out of nothing. Daniel is a man, and men have needs. If you aren't fulfilling those needs for him, of course he will go someplace else to seek them."

I can't even find words. How can my feelings mean nothing to her? Daniel has made me feel completely ugly and worthless. And yet this is...my fault? I sit in silence, the hot tears stinging my cracked cheeks as they cascade down my face. I suck in a sharp breath. I don't want her to know she's made me cry.

Marge sighs angrily on the other line. "I have been married to Frederick for forty-two years. I know what I'm talking about. He hasn't always been faithful but sometimes in order for a marriage to succeed, you need to look the other way. Now call my son and end this stupidity."

I stare at the phone in my hand for several minutes. I can't believe that just happened. I've always gotten along with my in-laws. I remember Daniel is still on the other line and return the phone to my ear.

"I'm back." I struggle to control my voice.

"What did she need?" Daniel asks.

I still can't find the words through my shock and my anger. "Call your mom and ask her," I say. I hang up and chuck the phone across the room.

Chapter Four

I pull up to my sister-in-law's brown brick rambler. The kids are practically bouncing out of their seats with anticipation. The front door opens and Melissa steps out. The kids all run into her outstretched arms. All except Danny and Olivia, who are too cool for that. They politely give their aunt a hug and move past her into the house.

"The boys are playing in the backyard," she says. "Go ahead and join them." Once the kids are all out of sight, Melissa throws her arms around my neck. I stumble a little at the unexpected gesture. "I'm so sorry," she whispers against my neck. "I'm sorry my stupid brother is putting you through this. Please don't give up on him. He really is a good man. I know he's trying so hard. Please don't give up on him yet. Remember all the good times?"

"Right now, no, I can't." I pull away from Melissa and kick a pebble on the cement.

"This truly is the drug of our time," she continues, shaking her head. "I know of so many failed marriages with porn as the culprit."

I'm not sure how to respond to this. After the phone call from his mother, I was afraid Daniel's entire family was going to hate me for kicking him out. And possibly blame me for not being more reasonable or whatever about his problem. I was not expecting his sister to be on my side. I realize I haven't responded yet, so I nod my head and shove my hands in my pockets. "Thanks for watching the kids tonight."

"It's not a problem at all. I'm just glad you're going with him. He was so scared to ask you. Not that I would have blamed you if you had said no," she clarifies. "I'm willing to watch them anytime you and Daniel need to go to therapy, or anything. I'm here to help."

"Thank you." Anytime you need to go to therapy? This isn't going to be a one-time thing, is it? For some reason, I'm just now realizing this could be a very long journey, mentally, physically, and financially. I don't want to sit through therapy every week. There's nothing wrong with me. Maybe this was a mistake. I'm about ready to grab my kids and run away screaming when Daniel pulls up. I sigh and look at Melissa. She offers me an encouraging smile and one more quick hug. Then she disappears inside, leaving me alone with him. The nervous pit in my stomach resembles an awkward blind date, except it's with my husband. It feels like I haven't seen him in ages.

As Daniel steps from his car I can't help but gasp. He looks awful! His shoulders sag. His skin seems to hang on his normally muscular frame. He has lost a lot of weight and it has definitely been too fast. His face is pale and sunken. His eyes look hollow with dark circles under them. Daniel offers me a forced half-smile. I try to smile in return. Do I look that bad, too?

He reaches out to open the passenger door for me.

"I got it," I say quickly, climbing in.

"I can't even get your door anymore?"

"I'm fine," I say.

Daniel's shoulders slump. He comes around the front of the car and climbs in. "Your hair looks really nice," he says, his eyes darting between me and the dashboard.

I subconsciously reach up and touch it. I almost forgot he hasn't seen me yet. "Thanks," I mumble. "I know you always prefer me with long hair, but..."

Daniel cuts me off. "You're beautiful," he says.

We sit awkwardly for several minutes as he drives into downtown Seattle.

"So tell me exactly what we're doing tonight," I finally say. "Am I supposed to just sit and listen? Is therapy for you or for both of us?" I steal a glance at Daniel. Even though his face is pale and his cheeks are hollow, sitting this close I can still see his chiseled jawline. Daniel catches me looking at him and I quickly turn away.

"I'm not exactly sure," he says. "This office was recommended to Melissa by a friend. I'm not certain if her friend saw this exact therapist or not. Just that she's supposed to specialize in both addictions and couples therapy."

"So it's for both of us then?"

He shrugs. "I guess."

The hair on the back of my neck stands on end. I feel like I've walked into a trap. "You didn't tell me we were going to couples therapy! I thought I was just coming along to listen to you talk to someone."

"I'm not sure," Daniel says. "But don't you think our marriage needs help, too?"

"Fine, I guess. But you're the one who broke it."

I pull the covers over Jaxon's sleeping form and tiptoe from the room. I trudge to my own room and collapse onto the bed. All five kids are sleeping. Finally! Daniel is late getting home, as always. I think he said they were taking a client out for dinner after work. Or maybe he has a night class tonight. I can't keep his excuses straight anymore. I pull the covers up under my chin and close my eyes. I still need to go downstairs and clean the mountain of dishes that are piled in the sink. I'm not sure I can even stand right now. I spent all morning baking eight dozen cupcakes for the school's bake sale. Then after the twins' dentist appointments and a PTA meeting, I had to pick up Olivia and Danny from school and rush them off to soccer and dance. We were so busy this afternoon, Jaxon missed his nap and was screaming by dinner. I pull Daniel's pillow over and bury my face under it. Dinner burned while I tried to break up a fight. The kids complained and refused to eat it. Then Maddy had an accident and peed all over the kitchen floor. By the time all the kids were bathed and in bed, it was thirty minutes past bedtime.

Daniel comes into our room, reeking of stale coffee mingled with sweat.

"Where have you been?" I ask, trying to sound casual.

"Work," he huffs, pulling off his shoes.

"It's late."

"I know it's late, but someone has to bring home the money so you can spend it all," he says angrily.

I'm too tired to fight. I lay his pillow back in his spot and close my eyes.

Daniel lays beside me on the bed and immediately puts his hand up my shirt and starts kissing the back of my neck. I roll over to face him.

"Daniel, I'm too tired."

"Come on, baby, I'll be quick. I have this new position I've been dying to try." Daniel describes what he wants me to do and eagerly begins unbuttoning my shirt.

His description causes the bile in the back of my throat to surface. My stomach swims with anxiety. I push his hands away and stand from the bed. "Daniel, I'm too tired and even if I wasn't, I have no interest in doing that. It sounds disgusting."

Daniel grunts and rolls onto his back. "I knew I should have married Kelly," he mumbles. Almost immediately, he begins to snore loudly.

I back out of the room quietly and walk downstairs to clean the kitchen. The sting of his words follow me.

Daniel parks beside a large business building. I stare up at the magnitude of the skyscraper while he gets out and comes around to open my door. I jump out before he can reach me. I feel even smaller surrounded by large buildings on all sides. I guess I haven't been to the city in a while. Daniel reaches for my hand out of habit, and then pulls back quickly when I snatch my own away. "Sorry," he mumbles.

I pretend it didn't happen and begin walking up the sidewalk, toward the entrance doors. We enter the large foyer, brightly lit by a huge chandelier hanging overhead. I can't help but stare up into all the tiny, fake crystals as we approach the wall directory. Daniel scans the names with his finger, landing on a Deborah Ferguson, LMFT. "Looks like we need to go upstairs," he says.

I feel fine until we step off the elevator and stand face to face with the therapist's office door. What if I go in there and see someone I recognize? What if they know why I'm here? This is so embarrassing.

Daniel holds the door open for me and I force my feet forward. I glance around quickly at the others in the waiting room. Everyone seems to be avoiding eye contact. Okay, good, no one is watching and silently judging me and my husband for being here. The receptionist hands Daniel a clipboard of paperwork and questionnaires. I sit beside him on the couch and stare at the wrinkles on the back of my hand while his pen scratches along the pages.

I pull out my phone and check my e-mail. Rolling my eyes, I open the one new message.

Dear Sarah,

Be honest with your husband. I know you're still angry, but share all the emotions you are feeling with him, both good and bad. If you are not honest and vulnerable with him, he cannot be honest and vulnerable with you.

Sincerely, a friend

"What's that?" Daniel asks, glancing over my shoulder.

I turn the phone off and shove it back in my purse. "Nothing," I shrug. "Just some junk e-mail."

He nods and goes back to his paperwork. So much for honesty.

"Daniel?" A formidable woman with short, spiky blonde hair approaches us from behind. We both turn in our seats and look at her. "I'm Deborah." She extends her hand and he shakes it. I reach out a hand as well, but she immediately drops her hand to her side and doesn't even look my way. "Follow me back to my office and we can talk."

Daniel holds his hand out in front of me. "My wife is coming in, too. I was told that's okay."

She finally glances in my direction, looking me up and down with swift, narrowed eyes. "If that's what you want," she says. She then turns on her heel and walks at a brisk pace through some glass doors. I feel like I have to jog to keep up. She holds the door open and then offers us each a seat.

I step further into the room and settle into a roomy, black armchair. Daniel sits in an identical one beside it, but he doesn't get comfortable. He sits on the edge with his hands on his knees, legs bouncing a mile a minute. Deborah clicks the door behind us. I squirm in the hot leather seat as she sits across from us in an office chair on wheels and leans forward toward Daniel.

"So tell me why you're here," she says.

Daniel takes a deep breath. "I am a sex addict," he says. "I have struggled on and off with pornography for more than half my life."

"And does that include masturbation?" she asks. Her voice is loud and sharp. I want to ask her to use her indoor voice like I would one of my kids. Doesn't she know how embarrassing this is? We don't want other people to hear!

Daniel hangs his head. "Yes."

"So when did it start?"

"When I was fourteen."

"And how often have you viewed porn and been masturbating since then?"

Daniel's eyes flit in my direction. "At least once a month. Lately it's been more like several times a week, almost daily. When we were first married, I had my longest sobriety of three months, but then I fell back into old habits."

My heart begins beating so hard and fast, I can feel its vibrations in my throat. At least once a month for fifteen years of marriage? And then lately it's been even more than that? How could I have not known? My entire marriage has been a lie. The tears start and I can't stop them.

"Tell me why you're here, then."

Daniel looks startled by the question. "I thought that's what I was telling you."

"Yeah, yeah, you have a problem with porn. So does 80 percent of men on this planet. But they aren't all in my office now, are they?"

"I guess not," Daniel says slowly.

"Why are you *here?*" she emphasizes the last word.

"I don't want to be addicted anymore," Daniel says, wringing his hands. "It's taken over my life, my job, my relationships." He glances at me briefly again.

"There we go!" Deborah claps her hands together and sits back farther in her chair. "Honesty! Finally! And from an addict, no less. So, you want to be cured from this addiction?"

"More than anything," Daniel says.

"Well, I'll believe it when I see it. Lots of addicts come to me with this problem, mostly to appease their wives. Few of them put in the work to truly recover and keep coming back."

Daniel slumps back in his chair. His face twitches. I know that look. He's trying to keep his emotions in check.

"Let me guess. You probably have ADD and, at least in part, blame that on your addiction?"

"Well, I… "

"I have news for you Daniel. Not all men who suffer from ADD struggle with addictions."

Daniel does have ADD and it's always been a sore spot for him to talk about. I don't know what made her bring it up. He certainly didn't.

"Almost 80 percent of men in America view porn regularly. Repeat that after me, Daniel," Deborah says, her thin mouth pressed in a firm line.

He looks to me and I shrug. He hesitates briefly before repeating her words. "Almost 80 percent of men in America view porn regularly."

"I am a sex addict."

He stares at her blankly.

"Repeat it, Daniel."

"I am a sex addict."

"I have destroyed my brain through my pornography addiction."

"I have destroyed my brain through my pornography addiction."

"I am incapable of feeling empathy and other important emotions."

I watch as Daniel repeats several more phrases after the therapist. His jaw is tight, and I can see a slight twitch under his right eye. I notice his knuckles are white from gripping the arms of the chair so tightly. I have no idea how he's holding it together. I thought Daniel deserved to be treated this way, after everything he's put me through. I was wrong. How can an addict possible get help when he's being verbally assaulted? I'm impressed Daniel is keeping it together. I would either be fighting back or crying by now.

The doctor continues to tell him how she doesn't really believe he wants to recover, because all addicts lie. He's going to have to prove himself to her. Our meeting is almost over and not once has Deborah looked my way or even acknowledged my existence in the room. When she's done belittling him, she finally turns to me.

"Do you have any questions, Mrs. Dunkin?"

I wipe my eyes and clear my throat. "What do I need to do? For myself?"

"Oh, honey, this has nothing to do with you! You don't need to do a thing."

Her words vocally punch me in the gut. So I'm supposed to just stay this miserable and screwed up? Awesome. Deborah stands and holds the door open for us. I cannot walk out of there fast enough. When Daniel and I both get back into our car, we each let out a huge sigh. After sitting in silence for a moment, Daniel looks up at me. "So?" he asks. "What did you think?"

"I think that woman needs some sensitivity training." I say.

Daniel grins.

"What a condescending, rude jerk! She was awful!"

Daniel's smile broadens. "I was afraid you would be happy with the way she talked to me."

"Are you kidding me?" I ask, my voice rising. "I want you to get better! Not become suicidal! What kind of a therapist talks so rudely to her patients? And on the first visit? And what was that about this not being my problem? We are married. What you do affects me. I can't believe she doesn't think I need some kind of help and healing as well."

Daniel reaches across the seat and takes my hand in his. "I love you." The heat in my cheeks begins to lessen and I take several deep breaths. I look at Daniel and we share a smile.

"I don't want to quit therapy," Daniel says.

"I don't want you to."

"But I never want to see that horrible woman again."

"Me neither!"

"I'll start calling around and find someone new tomorrow."

"That sounds like a great idea."

Daniel starts the car, but he doesn't return my hand. When I'm calm and realize he's still holding it, I fake a cough and pull my hand away to cover my mouth. I can see his face fall, but I keep my hand tucked under my thigh as we drive to pick up the kids.

Chapter Five

*D*ear Sarah,
Sometimes one therapist may not be the right one for you or your situation. Don't let this discourage you! Keep looking until you find one both you and your husband are comfortable with. Don't give up.

Sincerely, a friend

This is seriously starting to creep me out. How does this person know intimate details about my life? I haven't told anyone about the awful therapist experience. I haven't felt much like talking about it. I haven't felt much like talking at all. But I knew it would come out sooner or later. I look in the mirror at my round, green eyes and dab on one more brush of mascara.

"Kids, get in the car!" I yell. I'm having lunch with Breanna again today. Twice in one week is like a new record for us. I know the therapist story will come out. She knows me too well to allow something that juicy to remain a secret.

I can hear arguing downstairs over shoes. "I'm taking you to McDonalds for lunch. If I hear any fighting, I will order you a salad with no drink and no fries!" Silence. Behold the beauty of bribery. It helps that we almost never eat out, so my kids know this is their only chance for greasy French fries in the foreseeable future.

I grab an extra diaper and toss it into my crumb-lined purse before dashing down the stairs. I wish my lunch date didn't have to be at a McDonalds and I really wish it didn't have to be with five little sidekicks, but my mom was busy and I really feel like I need to talk to Breanna again.

At least four times in the last two days, Olivia or Danny have called for me repeatedly before I even heard them. Yesterday, Olivia asked what I had been staring at. Was I staring aimlessly at the wall again? I have no recollection of what I was staring at or where my thoughts were taking me. I've got to find a way to snap out of this funk, so Breanna offered to buy me lunch. I suggested the play place so hopefully we can actually get through a conversation. We'll see.

Bre waves happily as she enters the noisy, sticky room of terror. I wave from my mustard yellow table and offer her a seat across from me. Handing her a disinfecting wipe, I smile and tell her to take a seat. She laughs and accepts the wipe. She glances around before looking at me. Her smile fades and her voice drops.

"Where are the kids?"

I wave to the brightly colored tubes above our heads. "Somewhere up there, crawling around like little gerbils, I'm sure."

"Even the older two?"

I point to the row of computers across the room. Olivia and Danny are engrossed in whatever game is on the screen. Breanna turns back to me. "Awesome. Okay, so tell me about this awful therapist."

I rub my eyes and shake my head at the horrible memory. "I'm honestly not sure how he survived that. She wasn't even talking to me, and I wanted to do one of two things."

Breanna looks at me expectantly with raised eyebrows.

"I either wanted to punch her in the face or go home and kill myself."

Breanna's eyes widen in surprise. "Wow. That bad, huh?"

"I don't think it could possibly have been worse. I'm not sure where she got her degree, or if that tough therapy works on some people, but it absolutely did not work for my husband. I'm mad at him, but even I wanted to jump up in his defense."

"Do you think that was her plan?"

"No, she told me straight out that this has nothing to do with me and there's basically nothing I can do. Not only did she make Daniel feel worthless, but she made me feel invisible."

Breanna reaches across the table and puts a hand over mine. A silent tear slips down my cheek and I wipe it away.

"Hi, Mom! Mommy, look at me!"

I glance up and plaster a goofy smile on my face. Maddy is waving at me through the clear plastic tube over my head. Her cheeks are pushed up against the side, leaving a smudge. I wave back. Breanna looks up and waves as well. Soon Addy and Jaxon are at her side, fighting for our attention. We both smile and blow kisses. They giggle and disappear down a dark slide.

Once they're out of sight, Breanna turns her attention back to me. "Sarah, listen up, this therapist was a joke. They are not all that bad. I promise! Please give it another try." She stares at me with her big, brown, puppy-dog eyes until I have no choice but to agree.

I groan. "You are way too good at that."

She grins wickedly, "I know."

"Mommy, French fry?" Jaxon grabs my arm and pulls himself up onto my lap. He begins dousing his fry in ketchup, sucks it off, and then dips the soggy fry again. After three dunks, he finally eats the fry and goes for a second. Breanna looks at me with raised eyebrows and I shrug in return. Our conversation is momentarily suspended. After several fries and a long drink from his pop, Jaxon jumps from my lap and disappears into a purple tunnel.

Breanna looks at me and laughs. "He doesn't know the meaning of the word slow, does he?"

"Nope. In fact, none of my kids do. They're all on the go all day long."

Breanna's smile turns into a firm line. "I want you to start coming with me to group."

"Group of what?" I ask, taking a bite of my salad.

"It's a support group for women whose husbands or loved ones have a sex addiction like pornography. Some are still married, some are divorced, but we all come together to offer love and support during healing."

"You want me to go sit around with a bunch of complete strangers and tell them about my problems? Are you insane?"

"It seems strange at first, I admit, but you have no idea how therapeutic it can be to talk to other women in your same position. Your therapist was a quack. You *do* need to heal. You need to heal and Daniel needs to heal before you can ever start healing your marriage as a team. You're not alone in this, Sarah, but cutting yourself off from the world isn't the answer. You'll just become bitter and angry."

I stand up too fast and bash my knee against the bottom of the small, plastic table. I bite back the throbbing pain and stare Breanna in the face. "I'm allowed to be angry and bitter!" I say, my cheeks reddening. People in the play place are all looking at me, so I sit back down in a huff. Lowering my voice I say, "My husband cheated on me with images for almost fifteen years. The worst part is he lied to me about it. He made me feel completely inadequate and worthless." I spit out the words. "If I can't even trust my own husband, how do you expect me to trust complete strangers?"

"Mom, are you okay?" Olivia's sweet, soft voice calms my fury. She wraps an arm around my shoulder and rests her head against me.

I kiss her forehead. "Yes, sweetie, I'm fine. Will you go get your brothers and sisters for me please? It's time to go home."

"Sarah, please don't leave!"

"It's almost Jaxon's naptime anyway," I say. I gather our wrappers and dump them in the nearby trash. I avoid eye contact with Breanna as I finish cleaning up.

"Please just think about it, Sarah," Breanna whispers. "The meetings are every Wednesday night at 7:00. There's even a couples group you can go to as well. I'll go with you and you don't even have to talk if you don't want to. Just come and listen."

My blood is boiling, and I'm not even sure why. I wish someone would let me off of this emotional roller coaster ride. I don't want to say anything I might regret, so I shake my head and continue to stare down at the greasy yellow table. When I look up again, Breanna is gone.

My hands are shaking and my legs feel as though they might give out on me at any time. Because our appointment is in the middle of the day this time, I'm meeting Daniel here. My kids are with my mom again, who isn't asking questions yet, but I know they're coming. I don't want to talk to my mom about this, but I'm afraid her imagination will come up with something so much worse.

I didn't see Daniel's car in the parking lot, but I don't want to wait outside in the drizzle. I reach for the small glass door, with our therapist's office name etched onto the glass. This building is much smaller than the other one, and far less foreboding. I glance at the small directory and begin the walk up two flights of stairs. I'm trying to kill time in hopes that Daniel gets here quickly. I don't want to sit alone with a stranger, answering awkward questions.

I round the last corner and push open the door for the therapist's office. Immediately I feel at home. The reception area is warm, with soft, gentle music playing in the background. The chairs and couch are large and inviting. The coffee table in the center of the room holds a vase with fresh flowers. I'm the only person waiting right now, which is the complete opposite from the cold, crowded office we went to last time.

I sit on the long brown couch and reach for a fitness magazine. The couch is as comfortable as it looks. I sink in and flip through the pages of happy, healthy people. There are no fashion magazines or tabloids in sight.

A young man, probably in his mid-thirties walks into the room. "Are you Mrs. Dunkin?"

"Yes."

He steps toward me with his hand outstretched. "Hi, I'm Ryan. It's so nice to meet you."

I return his handshake. "My husband isn't here yet."

"That's just fine. I'll be in my office, right down the hall with the door open. Walk in as soon as he gets here." He points which direction we should go and I let out a huge sigh of relief. He's not going to make me sit awkwardly alone with him. I return to the magazine until I hear the door open again and look up.

"I'm so sorry I'm late." Daniel rushes into the room, looking worse than ever. His hair is disheveled, the dark circles under his eyes have grown, which I didn't think would be possible, and he looks almost as thin as when we were first married. "Has Ryan come in already?"

"Yeah," I say, standing. "He told us to meet him in his office once we're both here." I drop the magazine and it slaps back onto the table. I lead the way down the hall with Daniel shuffling behind me.

"Sarah, wait." He says, stopping outside the office door.

I turn and face him, folding my arms across my chest.

"I talked to my mom."

My breath catches in my throat.

"I am so sorry she treated you that way," he says. "I don't even understand what she was thinking."

I fight back the tears and shrug. I don't want to talk about this right now. I step forward and continue into the office.

Ryan stands as soon as we both enter, a bright, warm smile on his face. He offers us seats and shakes my hand again before shaking Daniel's. We sit on the offered couch, a cushion between us. I pick up a throw pillow and hold it on my lap, playing with the tassels on one end while Ryan speaks.

"How long have you two been married?"

"Fifteen years," Daniel answers.

"And how long have you known about your husband's addiction?" Ryan asks, looking at me.

I glance up. I was expecting to be a witness to therapy again, not a participant. Daniel begins to answer when Ryan puts a hand up to stop him. He looks at me again and smiles.

"Well, I guess I knew about it before we got married, but at the time my husband made it seem like something from his past. I thought it was a dumb mistake from his teens, something most teenage boys get into at one point or another."

"I'm going to stop you right there. Pornography is rampant in our society today, there's no doubt about that. But there is nothing normal about it. Recent studies have shown that pornography has the same effect on the brain as cocaine. A pornography addiction does many of the same things to our brain as hard drugs. We need to get out of this mindset that 'boys will be boys' or that 'porn is harmless.' Unfortunately, because it's everywhere, the statistics are no longer if a child will see pornography, but when. Both boys and girls. Now, I'm sorry I interrupted you. Please go on."

I feel suddenly validated by what Ryan has said. The hardest thing about this addiction is I don't feel like I can talk about it to anyone. Most people who think porn is normal don't understand the pain and sorrow it brings to a relationship. His mother is proof of that. It's such a taboo subject, I have to be careful about who I confide in.

Ryan is so different than our last therapist. I feel instantly comfortable opening up to him. I give him a small smile before continuing. "So I guess Daniel told me, but he didn't really tell me. I didn't understand that it's an actual addiction. I was sure he'd be done with it as soon as we got married and he had a real woman. Then several years ago, I found an image on his computer and he promised me he wouldn't look at porn again. I had no idea this was an ongoing problem until I caught him last week and asked him to leave. I kept thinking something was off in our marriage, but I couldn't put my finger on what it was. Now I understand."

Ryan nods his head and looks at Daniel. "Do you have anything to add?"

"I never wanted to hurt anyone, especially Sarah. I've been trying to quit for years. I kept convincing myself it was a bad habit and I could stop." Daniel lays his head in his hands and his shoulders begin to shake.

"I can't stop. No matter how much I hate it, no matter how awful I feel afterwards, I just can't stop."

Ryan hands Daniel a tissue and pats him on the shoulder. "Well, Daniel, you can't stop on your own because this is an addiction. Actually, the definition of addiction is habitual psychological and physiological dependence on a substance or practice beyond one's voluntary control. Addicts don't choose to be addicts. Most of the time they want to stop. But they've rewired their brains so they are no longer capable of making rational decisions. And most addicts cannot stop on their own. They need intervention of some kind whether it be a support group, therapy, or even rehab."

Daniel's shoulders slump, but Ryan smiles and places a hand on his shoulder again. "The good news, Daniel, is there's hope! You are here—that's a great start. And your beautiful wife is by your side. That's an even better start. You can do this, Daniel. It's not going to be easy or fun, but with the right tools, you absolutely can overcome this addiction and get your life back."

Daniel looks up at Ryan and wipes his nose with the back of his hand. "What do I need to do?"

Ryan chuckles. "I love your eagerness, but before we get started, we need to establish a couple of things. I know you're separated right now, which is a great idea for a lot of couples. It gives you time and space to heal as individuals."

He looks at me again. "Sometimes that separation is just the push some men need to clean up their lives. Others are able to stay together while they work through their own recoveries. Every couple is different. I'm glad you found something that will work for you. Okay, when we start with new couples in this program, we ask that you take divorce off the table for one year. Give us one year, and then you can re-evaluate your situation and make another decision at that point. Does that sound reasonable to you?"

The thought of divorce worries me more than the idea of going back to school or getting a job. I don't even know what I would do to try and support a family on my own. Daniel looks at me, and we both nod and say yes.

Ryan reaches into a cabinet beside his desk and pulls out a spiral-bound notebook. Folding back a couple pages of the notebook, he then hands it to me. "If it's okay with the both of you, I'd like to talk to Daniel on his own for a moment. Then I'd like to talk to you, Sarah. Then I'll bring you both together and we'll talk with the three of us once again."

My heartbeat quickens. Why does he need to talk to me alone?

"Sarah, I want you to read over this page and put a check next to anything that applies to how you have been feeling. Then we'll talk about it together in a few moments. If you want to have a seat in our reception area, I'll be out for you in about ten minutes."

I pick up the notebook and my purse and return to the comfy couch. The instructions say to place a check next to any of the trauma responses I have experienced due to my partner's addictive behavior. As I begin to read through the list of symptoms, my skin tingles and my face grows hot. I can check almost every single one.

— Fear and/or anxiety

— Outbursts of anger or rage

— Sadness and/or depression

— Hyper-vigilance (excessive alertness or watchfulness)

— Irritability

— Worrying or ruminating

— Intrusive thoughts of the trauma

— Tendency to isolate oneself

— Difficulty concentrating or remembering

— Feelings of panic or feeling out of control

— Increased need to control daily experiences (cleaning, parenting)

— Difficulty trusting; feelings of betrayal

— Feelings of self-blame or responsibility

— Flooding of feelings and/or emotional numbness

— Feelings of helplessness

— Minimizing the experience

— Feelings of detachment

— Concern about burdening others with problems

— Weight loss or weight gain

- — Feelings of worthlessness or being broken
- — Shock and disbelief
- — Diminished interest in everyday activities
- — Avoiding other people
- — Only sharing superficially
- — Preoccupation with body image
- — Difficulty falling or staying asleep

After I'm done checking off most of the symptoms, I scan the list again. I'm not sure whether to laugh or cry. I want to cry because I'm such a mess, but the thought that so many other women have felt the same things I am currently feeling fills me with hope. Maybe I'm not as crazy as I feared.

I read through the introduction pages of the support guide. I feel like I'm starting to get a better sense of this addiction. Thinking about it as an addiction and not just a bad habit he was choosing over me and my family really helps.

I'm so engrossed with all the facts and studies they've done on pornography, that I don't even notice when Ryan walks in. He just stands there, beside my chair, waiting patiently. I jump when I glance up and see him grinning at me.

"Sorry," I say, my cheeks turning pink. "This is just interesting."

"I'm glad you see it that way," Ryan says. "Some wives are so angry when they first get here, they aren't willing to learn about the addiction." Ryan motions for me to follow him and I oblige. I pass by Daniel in the hall. He seems more relaxed. That's a good sign. I return to the oversized couch in Ryan's office and pick up my comfort pillow again. I begin braiding the tassels together.

Ryan sits across from me and clasps his hands together. "Tell me how you are doing."

I glance up at Ryan. His face is friendly but his eyes are serious. "I'm…" Suddenly there's a lump in my throat. I attempt to swallow it down, but the lump moves up and bursts out my eyes instead. "I'm okay," I sniffle. I wasn't expecting this. The last therapist had no interest in me at all.

"It's okay to be upset," Ryan says in a calming voice. "You've been through a great ordeal. Why don't we go over that checklist I had you look at?"

I slide the workbook out and flip back to the checklist. I don't know why I feel embarrassed over the amount of them that are marked. Ryan looks through them and nods. "Do you know what these mean?" he asks, closing the book and handing it back to me.

"That I'm a mess?" I say, trying to make a joke.

Ryan humors me by smiling. "This means you're suffering from PTSD," he says.

I just stare at him blankly. "What? Isn't that something just war veterans get? Like soldiers who have seen and lived through horrific battles?"

"Yes, many war veterans also suffer from PTSD. It's true. But so can anyone who has experienced great trauma. You, Sarah, have lived through an extremely emotionally traumatic event. Your husband, the one person in the world you love and trust above all others, betrayed you. He kept a secret from you for fifteen very long years. Now you're questioning everything you thought to be true in your life."

"Geez, are you a therapist or a psychic?"

Ryan smiles. "I've seen and helped many couples just like you. From what I can tell so far, you and Daniel stand a very good chance of recovering your marriage."

I shift in my seat, staring down at my braiding handiwork. "What makes you say that?"

"First of all, you're both here. That means you both want to work it out. Secondly, I sense a lot of sadness from both of you, but not a ton of anger. I'm sure you're angry. It's healthy to feel that and you have every right to. But those who struggle the most with recovery cling to that anger. They dwell in the anger so long that they allow it to control everything and they never move past it. They never experience other equally important emotions."

"So what do we need to do?" I ask. "To heal and feel like a husband and wife again."

"Well, before you can even begin working on your marriage, you need to heal as individuals first. Daniel needs to get a good grasp on his addiction and remain sober, while you need to do a great deal of self-care. You need to take care of you."

"I'm not even sure how to do that," I admit without looking up.

"You're a mom, right?"

I nod. "We have five."

Ryan's eyes widen briefly. "Most moms struggle with self-care. You're so busy taking care of everyone else that you forget about yourself."

I nod again. "That's just what moms do."

"Let me tell you an analogy. You're familiar with riding on airplanes?" he asks.

"Yes."

"Okay. When the stewardess is going over all the safety tips, she talks about what to do if the air masks drop down. Do you remember?"

"Yeah, you put on your own first, and then put the mask on any children sitting beside you."

"And why is that? Doesn't that seem selfish?"

"No, because you can't help the child if you're dead."

Ryan's smile broadens to cover his entire face. His analogy clicks. "So now you understand?" he asks.

"It's easier to understand than it is to carry out, but I will try. I can't be of any use to my children if I'm emotionally dead."

"Precisely."

"So what exactly does self-care entail?"

"That depends on the individual," Ryan says. "Many women benefit from a support group. We hold one here every week. Anyone is welcome to attend."

My heart drops into the pit of my stomach. Breanna flashes in my mind.

"Find something that makes you happy. Write, read, paint, go for long walks, get a pedicure, just do something for you every single day. As hard as that can be for moms, especially temporary single moms, you can't heal if you don't take care of yourself. Meditation can be very beneficial as well. Take a few moments to find peace and quiet in your daily life."

This recovery thing sounds time consuming. Where am I going to find time to pick up a hobby and meditate?

"It's very important for you to establish a good support group. Whether it be trusted friends, family, or even a support group of strangers, you need to find people you can go to and talk things out with. You can't heal if you keep all your feelings bottled up inside."

The more Ryan talks, the more I feel like a complete jerk for the way I treated Bre, who's been my only support group so far.

Ryan claps his hands together and stands. "All right, I'll go grab Daniel and we can all talk together now."

I sigh. More talking? I want to collapse into the cushions and fall asleep. All this talking has me completely drained emotionally. I don't think I can cry another tear right now if I tried.

Chapter Six

*D*ear Sarah,
    It's time to find a support group. You need other women who have been in your same position and can relate to the things you are feeling. You will learn more from them than you ever thought possible, and they will be privileged to learn from you. Don't be afraid. You're not alone.

    Sincerely, a friend

    All right, enough already! First Breanna, then the therapist, and now my mysterious internet friend is telling me to talk about my problems with other people. Leave the poor dead horse alone.

    Fine. I'll call Breanna.

    I pull out my phone and grumble. This is so unnatural. Besides, maybe Breanna won't even want to take me anymore. I was really rude to her last time we were together and I haven't heard from her since. At least I don't think I've heard from her … unless she's my mystery friend. I pause and think about it for a minute. How would she have known before I told her? I guess she is friends with Daniel, but I can't imagine him confiding in a woman about this addiction. I shake my head and stare at Breanna's number in front of me. "Here goes nothing," I say and push call.

I stare up at the large brick church building in front of me. My feet become heavier and heavier with each additional step. I pause on the sidewalk and bend over, sticking my head between my knees. With my hands resting on my legs, I suck in as much air as I can. My chest feels tight, my head is swimming, and I feel like my dinner could make a reappearance at any time.

I feel a warm hand on my back. "Slow down, Sarah, don't make yourself sick," Breanna whispers quietly. She remains by my side, rubbing my back until I straighten. "Remember," she says, "This is your first time. You don't have to share. No one is expecting you to. Just observe and listen. Then you can decide if and when you want to come back."

I nod and grit my teeth. Now I understand why she insisted on picking me up. If I'd driven myself, I don't think I would have even made it out of the car.

Breanna moves ahead of me and pulls open the heavy wooden door. I follow closely behind her, watching her red heels as we walk. I avoid looking at anyone. What if someone recognizes me?

All too soon Breanna stops and I almost crash into her. She points to an open door and steps inside. The room is bigger than I expected, with simple white walls and a large picture of Christ in a gold frame hanging from the center of the back wall. At least I'm pretty sure it's a picture of Christ. My family has never been much for going to church. There's a small table pushed up against the wall, directly below the picture. The table holds two water pitchers, a coffee maker, and some cups. I move toward the table and pour myself a glass of water from one of the pitchers. Placing the Styrofoam cup to my lips, I drink the entire thing in one gulp. I'm suddenly ridiculously thirsty and pour two more glasses before turning around to find a seat by Breanna. There are about a dozen folding chairs forming a circle in the center of the room. Breanna smiles warmly and waves me over. I hand her one of the cups and sit down. We're the first ones in the room.

A short while later two women enter, wearing attractive suits and perfect manicures. I'd guess they are super models, with the way they carry themselves, not to mention they're absolutely gorgeous. These women have husbands with a sex addiction? How is that possible? One of them looks my way and smiles. I realize I've been staring and quickly turn my attention to Breanna.

The next woman to walk in surprises me even more. She has to be at least seventy years old with beautiful snowy hair. She approaches us and gives Breanna a big hug before taking the seat on her other side. Breanna introduces us. I smile politely, but can't remember her name as soon as she says it. Another cluster of women enter the room and beeline for the table, making themselves coffee before sitting down. I can't imagine drinking caffeine right now. I'm jittery enough as it is.

A woman enters the room, holding a clipboard and looking very much in charge. She settles into the chair nearest the refreshment table and sets her things down. She glances at her watch and then clears her throat. Two more women rush into the room, offering apologies for their tardiness. Once everyone is seated, she clears her throat again. "Good evening, everyone, my name is Kelly."

"Hi, Kelly." I jump when the entire room says hello in unison.

"I'm your mediator for this meeting. Just to make sure you're in the right place, this is the family and spouses support group for sex addictions." Everyone nods so she goes on. "Do we have anyone here for the first time?"

My face explodes into a deep crimson. I slowly raise a trembling hand.

Kelly smiles in my direction. "Welcome. We hope you can find solace and support in our sisterhood here."

I nod and then stare down at my hands. I can feel ten pairs of eyes watching me.

"This is a safe place. We begin with a discussion, where the floor is open to everyone to ask questions or voice their concerns. Then we will go around the circle for sharing time."

My throat tightens. Breanna seems to sense my tension. She reaches over my lap and squeezes my hand.

"During sharing time, however, there is no cross-talk. We allow each woman to say whatever she feels inclined to share, with no judgements and no interruptions. And it is, of course, perfectly acceptable to pass."

I release a huge breath of relief.

"Our anonymity is essential, so please refrain from sharing any details about your personal life unless it pertains to the addiction or your recovery. Introduce yourself before you speak by stating your first name only. What you hear here, let it stay here."

"Here, here." I jump for the second time when the quiet room erupts in unison.

"The floor is now open if anyone has something they would like to discuss," Kelly says. She slips her clipboard under her chair and pulls her reading glasses up to rest on the top of her head.

I sit back with my arms folded across my chest and listen as the discussion moves from the best internet filters to keep our kids safe to the struggles of intimacy after this addiction is discovered. I squirm slightly in the plastic chair, which seems to be getting harder beneath me. I can't believe how open and frank these women are. And I can't believe how matter-of-factly they speak about pornography and the addiction. I still struggle with saying that word out loud. It's like a curse word that leaves a nasty aftertaste in my mouth.

One of the ladies mentions a WoPA while she is talking and I look at Breanna to explain, but she doesn't notice me. I raise my hand for the first time.

"I'm sorry, I don't mean to interrupt," I say. "But what's a whoa-puh?"

Kelly smiles. "Not a problem at all. Questions are always encouraged." She clears her throat. "It's a term we use a lot around here," she says. "A WoPA is an acronym. It stands for wives of porn addicts."

"Although it doesn't just encompass wives," one of the model-ladies pipes in. "I consider myself a WoPA, even though my addict is my boyfriend."

"That's true," Kelly says. "I've also heard it can stand for women of porn addicts. Some of us here are married, some are divorced, some are separated, some are dating, and some are mothers. But we are all WoPAs in that we all have or have had an addict that we care about. And we're all trying to overcome the emotional turmoil and hopelessness caused by our loved one's addiction."

The discussion moves on while I sit back and listen. When half an hour has passed, Kelly stands and announces it is time for the sharing portion to begin. "Who would like to start?" she asks.

"I will," Breanna says, raising her hand. Of course. I scrunch my nose and try to glare, but Breanna ignores me. With Breanna starting, that means my turn is next. I hoped I would have longer than this to decide if I want to share. My palms begin to sweat and my face grows hot.

"Hi, my name is Breanna."

"Hi, Breanna." I'm prepared this time, and even join in.

"I went on a date this last weekend. It was my first date since my divorce."

Everyone claps for Breanna and she smiles. I'm too stunned to join in. I stare at Breanna, my eyes widen. Her divorce was final almost two years ago. I can't believe she hasn't been on a date since then! I feel like the worst friend in the history of the world. How could I not know the reason for her divorce, her not dating, and now her first date?

"I've been asked out a number of times since my divorce, but I always turned the men down. After the shock of my husband's addiction, and then him choosing the addiction over me, I really wasn't ready to trust again. But I finally felt ready this time. So when the invitation came, I accepted it. I don't know if we'll go out again, but it was a really nice evening. He acted like a gentleman all night, we had good conversation, and we even laughed. At one point there was a kid sitting behind him at the movie theater, kicking his chair. It started causing a lot of anxiety because my ex would have completely lost his temper over something like that. But my date just turned around and made a joke. The kid laughed and stopped, and the incident was over before it began."

I watch Breanna's mouth continue to move but my own thoughts muffle her words. I can feel the heat creeping up my neck. Each breath becomes more labored. My hands begin to shake. I close my eyes and focus on getting air to my brain before the panic attack hits with full force.

Danny closes his math book and shoves his chair back. "Done!"

"Great job, bud. Will you run downstairs and grab two cans of green beans for dinner please?"

"But, Mom, I just worked for like an hour on homework. Can't I go play?"

"Sure, you deserve a break after all your hard work. In fact, I spent all day doing your laundry, so maybe I should just take a break instead of making you dinner, too."

Danny rolls his eyes. "Okay, I'll get the beans."

I chuckle once he's out of earshot. Addy and Maddy come screaming into the room, with Jaxon hot on their trail. "Mommy, Mommy, guess what?" Addy asks.

"What?" I try and ask with equal enthusiasm.

"We're super heroes!" They each pump a fist in the air and begin flying around the room.

Maddy grabs a towel from the drawer and asks for a cape. Once three clothespins are secured onto three towels, the flying off couches, and fighting of bad guys commences. The garage door opens and we all look over in surprise to see Daniel enter the kitchen.

"Wow, you're home early," I say.

"Can't a guy come home early without getting the third degree?" he asks.

"I was just excited to see you," I say.

Daniel walks over and kisses me lightly on the lips. "Sorry," he mumbles. "I have a lot of homework tonight, so I left the office a little early."

"Well, you're in time to join us for dinner." I have to speak loudly to be heard over all the squeals and hi-yahs.

"Sounds great," Daniel sighs. He pulls up a stool and watches the kids racing around the living room.

Danny appears and sets the two cans on the counter beside Daniel.

"Olivia, will you set the table for dinner, please?" I ask.

"Sure, Mom, just let me finish this last problem. I'm almost done."

Daniel pounds his fist on the kitchen counter. "IF YOUR MOTHER ASKS YOU TO DO SOMETHING, THEN DO IT!" he shouts. He jumps to his feet and grabs Olivia roughly by the arm, yanking her off the kitchen chair. "SET THE TABLE NOW!" Then, turning to the younger kids who stand frozen in the living room, he yells, "AND SHUT UP!"

I come around the counter and grab Daniel by the shoulders. "Get out," I hiss. "Go for a walk until you can calm down."

Daniel turns, grabs his car keys and slams the door behind him. I drop to my knees and pull a sobbing Olivia onto my lap.

"What did I do wrong?" she chokes out.

"Nothing, sweetie," I say, stroking her hair. I glance at the closed white garage door. I'm too stunned. I don't know what to do. "You didn't do anything wrong."

My breathing now under control, I peek open my eyes and try to refocus on what Breanna is sharing.

"I feel like this was a huge step for me and I'm grateful for this group and everything I've been taught. I'm glad I've found happiness and have been able to forgive my ex. I can't even imagine holding onto all those angry feelings. I don't want to be bitter. I want to be better."

I smile at Breanna, and then I realize everyone is looking at me expectantly. My cheeks flush and I shake my head. "Pass," I say.

"Would you at least share your name with us please?" Kelly asks.

"I'm Sarah."

"Hi, Sarah." I jump again. Dang it. It's really unnerving. I'm not sure I'll ever get used to it.

Each woman in the circle takes a turn sharing. I'm the only one who passes. As I listen to their stories, I'm not sure if I really belong here. Most of them have been coming for a couple months at least. And most of them seem really positive. Two of them even mention how grateful they are for the addiction itself. They go on to explain how overcoming the addiction together has made their marriage stronger than they ever thought possible. They wouldn't trade the experiences they've had, good or bad, for anything.

I'm not sure if I can ever feel that way. How can you be grateful for something so awful? There are plenty of experiences I wish I could trade or take back. Maybe everything is just too fresh for me, but listening to how great they are all doing doesn't help my mood. I feel irritable and wish just one person would complain, even for a second.

Finally the sharing comes to the old lady sitting on Breanna's other side. "Hi, I'm Julia."

"Hi, Julia."

"I've been married to my husband for forty-seven years. He's been addicted to pornography for forty-seven of those years."

My jaw drops open. I close it quickly, hoping no one noticed. No such luck. Julia points at me.

"I know what you're thinking," she says. "Why on earth would I stay with an addict for that long? Well, I was raised in a generation where divorce wasn't an option. And now, I don't want to have to explain why grandma and grandpa are divorcing to all my grandkids and great-grandkids. And through it all, I love my husband still. He's been in and out of rehab several times, but always seems to fall back into old habits after a year or two of sobriety. I've forgiven my husband countless times for the pornography, the strip clubs, and the affairs. Now that we're alone, we live in separate bedrooms. I know I'm not the best example to you ladies of what to do. These kinds of programs didn't exist even a few years ago, so I never had people to confide in. Maybe if I had, I would have learned how to be stronger. As it is, I've come too far to give up now. But there is one thing I can tell you with certainty.

"Don't let this addiction stop you from living your life. I have seven incredible children, who are all grown and married with kids and even some grandkids of their own. If I had slowed down my life to wait for him to recover, I might not have them all today. And you know what? Despite everything, I love my life! My children and grandchildren are my whole world. I am very close to each of my kids. My husband has never had a stable relationship with any of them. While he wallows in his room, consumed in self-loathing, I am living a beautiful life. Because I decided a long time ago that I was not going to let this addiction rule me. I will not allow it to dictate my life or my happiness. While my husband suffers, losing almost everything to this addiction, I am living a wonderful life, free of worry."

When the meeting ends, several ladies offer me a handshake and words of welcome. Many of them tell me to come back, promising it gets easier. I thank them all as I try and push Breanna out the door. Once in her car, I lean back and close my eyes.

"So?" she asks. "What do you think?"

"They are all very nice and very welcoming."

And?"

"And I think I'm in a totally different place. Everyone seemed so happy, it kinda pissed me off."

Breanna laughs. "It will get better," she says. "I promise. Every one of them has been exactly where you are right now. They understand the pain and the anger, trust me, even if they didn't talk about it. I really hope you decide to keep coming. You will learn more from them than you ever thought possible, and they will be privileged to learn from you. Don't be afraid. You're not alone."

I turn my head and stare at Breanna. Her words sound way too familiar. "Have you been sending me e-mails?" I ask.

She looks over at me, her brow wrinkled. "I text you almost every day. Why would I e-mail you?"

She didn't actually answer the question. "I don't know, because you're trying to be mysterious?"

Breanna laughs. "I'm sorry," she says, "but I have no idea what you're talking about!"

I study her face. Her brown eyes are looking straight back into my own. She doesn't seem to be lying.

"Can't you just see who the e-mail is from? It should have their name listed."

"There's no name. It's just listed as being from 'private.' And when I tried to reply, the e-mail bounced back to me saying it couldn't be sent. It's so weird!"

The amusement drops from Breanna's face. "This is starting to sound more than weird. It's creepy! What does this stalker write to you about?"

"The e-mails are all guidance and suggestions for dealing with this addiction. Whoever my secret friend is, they always have advice and words of hope. I get an e-mail almost every day. The first one started the morning after Daniel left."

"I'm sorry to disappoint, but it's really not me. I kinda wish I'd thought of it first though. And this person never gives any details about themselves or how you're connected?"

"Nothing."

"Hmmmm." Breanna pulls out of the parking lot and begins the drive back to my house. She thankfully seems to understand my need for silence. If Breanna isn't my secret friend, who else could it be? My thoughts drift back to group. My mind is swimming with information that I heard tonight. But the words that stand out the most are Julia's. "Don't let the addiction stop you from living your life."

Chapter Seven

The following week as we are walking out of therapy together, Daniel gently grabs my arm.

"Can we talk for a minute?" he asks.

I glance around before finally meeting his eyes. "Uh, sure. What is it?"

"How are things at home?"

"Well, school starts next week, so I'm super busy trying to do school shopping, get the kids back on a normal sleep schedule, and keep Danny from running away so he doesn't have to go back."

"What can I do to help?"

I almost choke. I don't even know how to answer. I'm so used to doing everything for the kids on my own, I can't think of what can possibly be passed off to him. But he's offering. I don't know the last time he made an offer like this.

"You know what would be the most helpful?" I ask, looking straight into his soft blue eyes. "Take each of the kids on a Daddy/daughter or Daddy/son date before school starts. They miss you and I really think some one-on-one time will lift their spirits and lessen their anxiety over the new school year. Unless, of course, you're too busy." Here it is: the moment of truth. The old Daniel, with work, school, homework, and his addiction, would definitely be too busy for four separate dates. He'd make an excuse, buy the kids off with a gift, and call it good. I glance down at my shoes so Daniel can't see the nervous way I'm biting my lip.

"Okay," he says.

I snap up and look into his smiling eyes. "Okay?"

"I might have to move some things around, but tell Olivia to plan on me picking her up tomorrow at 6:00 for dinner. She can choose the restaurant."

"I can't tell her if you're just going to back out."

"I won't back out," he says.

"Great, she'll be really excited." I start walking toward my car. I'm sure Melissa is pulling her hair out by now and is ready for me to come get the kids.

"Can I ask you one more thing?"

"Sure." I begin digging through my purse for my keys.

"Can I take you out to dinner next week, before therapy?"

"Like a date?"

"Yes." Daniel takes a step closer to me. "Will you please have dinner with me before therapy? I just want to talk. I … I miss you."

My heart is screaming inside. I miss him, too, at least the good parts. I shift from one foot to the other. I'm not sure if I'm ready. I bite my lip and fidget with the car keys in my hand. This is why we're going to therapy. I can't heal my marriage if I'm not taking steps in that direction. I sigh loudly. "All right. I'll check with Melissa when I pick up the kids and see if she can watch them longer next week."

"Thank you," he says. "I love you."

Daniel turns back toward his own car.

"Good luck in class tonight," I call after him.

He smiles and waves. I catch a glint of the man I used to know before unlocking my own door to leave.

I peek around the corner of my locker to steal another glance at Daniel. His tall, broad shoulders sit comfortably beneath his letterman jacket. His dark brown hair waves perfectly, swooping down just above his ocean-blue eyes. He says something and the three beautiful girls around him chuckle. We've been friends since junior high, but something changed over the summer. He's not just Daniel anymore. He's the gorgeous, blush-inducing, throat-drying boy of my dreams. If only he felt the same way. I smile and sigh to myself.

"In your dreams, Ginger." Kelly walks past me, sneering. Her short, green cheerleader skirt swishes around her tan thighs. Her curly blonde hair bounces as she approaches Daniel, looping her hand through the crook of his arm.

Daniel looks up and sees me watching him. I duck my head back inside the locker to cover the pink flushing my cheeks. I close the locker to find him standing right in front of me. Kelly and her friends glare in my direction.

"Sarah doesn't need to wait for her dreams," he says loudly. "She already has my heart."

He wipes Kelly's hand from his arm, like a squished bug. Taking my books in one hand, he wraps his arm over my shoulder and walks me to class.

A little to my dismay, Melissa is more than happy to watch the kids for longer next week so I can have dinner with Daniel. She seems overly enthusiastic about it and I can't help but wonder if I've been duped. She knew about the plan all along.

On the drive home, I turn down the radio. "Olivia, Dad wants to take you out to dinner tomorrow night, just you and him."

"Why?" she asks hesitantly.

"He misses you guys and wants to spend some time, just with you. He even said you can pick the restaurant."

"Really?" Her voice jumps with excitement.

"Yeah, so be thinking about where you want to go, okay?"

Olivia claps her hands together, her face beaming. I glance up at the roof. "Please don't disappoint her," I whisper. I glance in the rearview mirror and see Danny, sitting across from his sister with his arms folded, his lip turned down.

"You're next, Danny, so start thinking about where you want Dad to take you too, okay? He wants to take each of you out, one on one, before school."

Danny grunts.

"Jaxon, too?" His little voice is so full of hope.

"Daddy is just taking out the big kids before school starts."

Huge crocodile tears begin sliding down his cheeks. "Jaxon big kid."

"Oh, buddy." He sure knows how to make my heart break. "I'll talk to Daddy about your turn too, okay?"

Jaxon sniffles. "Okay."

Maddy yells from the back, "Do I have to share my turn with Addy?"

"I want to go together!" Addy yells.

"No! Just me and Daddy!" Maddy yells back.

"Together!" Addy wails.

"Addison and Madison, you will each have a turn and if you go on your own, you won't have to decide on a restaurant together. And you won't have to share Daddy."

They both cheer. Thank goodness it worked this time.

Olivia spends the next afternoon trying on all her new school clothes, deciding which outfit to wear for her special night with Dad. My heart swells and aches at the same time. When Daniel arrives, more dressed up than usual in a button up shirt and slacks, Olivia beams at him from the stairwell. Before she can walk to the front door, Daniel is mauled by three little monkeys who come flying in from the other room.

"Daddy!"

"Daddy!"

"Hold me!"

Daniel laughs. It's good to see some light return to his eyes, if only for a moment. He scoops the three of them up in one giant bear hug and squeezes until they all squeal to be released. Then he attempts to put them back on the ground. Maddy and Addy each grab an arm and try to climb him, like he's a giant tree. Jaxon begins to cry in his fight for attention. Daniel looks at me with pleading eyes.

I step forward, scooping up Jaxon in one arm while trying to pry Addy off her father with the other hand. "Come on, guys, dinner time. I made chicken nuggets and French fries."

The girls release their grips and race for the kitchen.

"I can eat more chicken than you! I want five pieces."

"I can eat six!"

"I can eat ten!"

"Cannot."

"Can too."

"Mom!"

I roll my eyes and wrap an arm around Olivia. "Have a great time, sweetie." She smiles back at me and waves to her little brother, and then follows Daniel out the door.

I settle Jaxon into his booster seat and dish up food for the three youngest before I go to the foot of the stairs and call Danny down for dinner. After three failed attempts, I sigh and lug my tired body up the thirteen steps and down the hall to his room. I knock before pushing the door open. Danny is laying on his bed with earbuds in, staring up at the ceiling. I walk over and pull the music from his ear. He jumps and looks up at me.

"Sorry, sweetie, you couldn't hear me. I think you've got that too loud."

Danny shrugs.

"Dinner is ready."

"Is Dad still here?"

"No, he and Olivia went to dinner."

Danny scoots to the edge of his bed and stands up. "Do I have to go tomorrow night?"

I pause in his doorway. "Why? Don't you want to go out to dinner with Dad? He offered to take you anywhere."

Danny shrugs again, his eyes are focused on a piece of loose carpet. He begins playing with it between his toes.

"I think you should go," I say. "You'll have fun, and it might be nice to get away for a couple hours before school starts. I know the twins have been driving you crazy lately. Why don't you want to go?" I cock my head to the side, trying to read a clue on his expressionless face.

"Fine, I'll go," he mumbles and stalks from the room.

I don't have too much time to worry about what's bothering Danny. My thoughts are interrupted by a crash and a scream downstairs. I run to clean up whatever mess has been made in my absence.

After a very loud dinner, I announce it's bath time. A reluctant Danny shuffles toward the shower.

"Use soap!" I remind him. I'm met with an eye roll. When did he suddenly become a sullen teenager?

After much fighting to get the younger three into the tub, and then even more fighting to get them out again, I help Jaxon dry off and get his pajamas on. Wet from all the little splashing hands, I turn to change when I hear screaming from the girls' room. I go in to find their naked little bodies dancing around the room, chasing each other with wet towels. After two swift spankings, they begin getting pajamas on while I go in my own room to finally change out of my wet clothes.

I sit on the edge of my bed to take a break for a few moments and open my phone. I have a new e-mail.

Dear Sarah,

Talk to your kids. Kids are smart. Even your youngest knows something isn't right. You get to determine how much you share with them, but they need to know their dad is still there for them. They need to know he is still a part of their lives. And they need to know whether or not he's coming home. Don't leave them to figure things out on their own. They need assurance and comfort right now. They need you.

Sincerely, a friend

I close my phone and lay back on my bed. I hate them for making me feel guilty, but I hate myself even more for losing my temper. I glance down at my hand. My eyes burn as I stare at the red coloring. The old me would have gotten a towel and joined in the fun. After all, they're just kids. They have no idea what's going on. Their lives shifted dramatically and no one has explained to them why. No wonder they've been so hyper and out-of-control lately. They don't know how to react because they don't know what's wrong. My stomach is twisting in knots as I walk back down the hall toward their bedroom.

Both girls are dressed, their eyes red from tears. I pull them each onto one leg of my lap and stroke their wet hair as I apologize and whisper words of comfort.

"Do you girls understand why Daddy isn't home right now?" I ask, looking into their emerald eyes. The twins were the only ones out of our kids who ended up with my green eyes and red hair. I love looking at them and seeing miniature versions of myself.

"You said Daddy is sick," Addy explains.

"Is he ever coming home?" Maddy asks, scrunching her eyes.

"Yes, Daddy is working really hard to get all better so he can come home. Does it make you sad or nervous that he's gone?" I ask.

"Jordan from Kindergarten says you're probably getting a divorce," Maddy says. "She said her Daddy left for a while and never came back."

"He lives with Tena now," Addy adds.

I sigh and glance up at the ceiling. Little kids are so honest, but sometimes so not helpful. "Daddy and I are not getting a divorce," I say. "We're just taking a little break while Daddy gets better. I just don't want you girls to be worried. Everything will be okay. All right?"

"Okay."

"Okay, Mommy."

"Can we have a story now?"

With my arms around them, I squeeze them together for one more hug. "Yes, you may each pick one book."

We read stories together on Maddy's bunk, and then I tuck them in bed. I find Jaxon asleep on his floor, curled up with a monster truck protectively tucked under one arm. I smile and carefully lift him into his red racecar bed. I lean over and kiss the top of his head. He still carries the faintest hint of baby smell. I'll be so sad when it's finally faded and gone. I kiss him again, my lips lingering on his soft warm skin. I know I shouldn't tempt fate any longer. I take one final sniff of his freshly washed head and tiptoe from the room.

As I make my way to Danny's room, I hear the front door open and close. I tell him goodnight and we share a laugh when I try to kiss him and he ducks. After a few minutes of playing this game, I pin his arms down and give him a big, sloppy kiss on his cheek. He groans but his face is smiling. Then I walk across the hall to Olivia's room. She's in her pajamas already, reading a book in bed.

"Did you have a good time?"

She beams. "Dad bought me steak!"

"What? No fair!" We both smile.

Olivia's face grows serious. "Mom, what's going on?"

My heart begins to race. Why oh why does my e-mail friend always have to be right? "What do you mean?"

"What's going on with you and Dad?"

My throat is dry, my hands sweaty. "I told you, babe."

"I know, but I don't believe you. If everything was fine and Dad was just sick or something, he would be home. Or at least you guys would be acting more normal."

"What do you mean?"

Olivia stares at me through squinted eyes. "You don't talk to each other. You don't kiss. You act weird whenever you have to see him. Are you guys getting a divorce?"

I sit on the edge of Olivia's bed and place her book back on her nightstand. I pick up her hand and hold it between my own. "No, your dad and I aren't getting a divorce. But you're right, there is something going on. Daddy is having some problems he needs to work through. We're going to a therapist together to try and work everything out. I know things are weird right now, and I'm really sorry about that. But your dad and I are really trying to work through it so we can stay married and hopefully Dad can come home again."

Olivia nods, but her chin quivers.

"How did you know Dad and I don't talk?"

"Because Dad kept asking about you all night. He asked how you are and if you're happy. Then we'd talk about something else and then like ten minutes later, he'd ask how you're doing again. If you guys were talking, he wouldn't have to ask me!"

"You're right, and I'm sorry."

"What kind of problems is Daddy having?"

I sigh. My mind races for the best answer. "It's kind of like Daddy is sick right now. His body isn't sick, but his mind is."

She looks at me between squeezed eyebrows.

I try again. "Do you remember when Jaxon was born, and he was really small and sick, so he had to stay in the NICU at the hospital for a few extra days? You guys weren't allowed to see him very much, but that was just because he needed some extra time to grow and get better. And now he's healthy and fine, and you can play with him every day. Well, that's kind of like your dad. He needs a break away from us, just for a little while, so he can have some time to heal and get better."

"Is there anything we can do to help him?"

My voice trembles. "We just need to keep loving him. Hopefully he can recover and come home soon."

Chapter Eight

The last several days, Daniel has kept his promise. It took a lot of coaxing on my part, but Danny did go to dinner with his dad. I'm not sure what's going on with him. He has always been a daddy's boy. Even when he was a baby, Daniel could soothe his cries better than I could. Now my son has begun to retreat from not only Daniel, but from the whole family. He came home from dinner fairly early and went straight to his room without a word.

Addy chose McDonalds for her special night out last night. I tried to hide my laughter when Daniel came to pick her up and she told him excitedly where she wanted to go. He visibly flinched. Daniel has never been able to stand how noisy and crowded that place is. But he smiled, scooped her up, and they had a grand time together. Addy spent so much time talking about the play place and the ice cream cone Daddy bought her for dessert that Maddy began to cry. He may have another McDonalds repeat tonight, if he's not careful.

The doorbell rings. I give the spaghetti sauce a good stir and then walk to the bottom of the stairs.

"Maddy, your dad is here! I hope you have your shoes on!" I've only been asking her to put them on for the last twenty minutes. No one comes racing this time so I sigh and walk towards the front door.

Daniel smiles at me. His coloring seems to be coming back a little. I think these date nights are helping more than just the kids.

"Hi," he says.

"Hi." I wipe my hands on my apron and check behind me for any signs of Maddy on the stairs.

"Are we still on for our date tomorrow night?"

I nod slowly, the knot in my stomach tightening. "Yeah, Melissa said she'd be thrilled to watch the kids. She even offered to take them overnight." I shake my head. "We should have just hired her to be our therapist."

Daniel shows the hint of a smile. "Yeah, I can see how that would go. 'Why can't you crazy kids just work this out? Kiss and make up already.'" He chuckles and I smile weakly at his impression of Melissa. He nailed it. Daniel clears his throat and I look down at my toes. They desperately need to be painted. I step over to the foot of the stairs again. "Maddy?"

She comes racing down, socks on, shoes in hand. I roll my eyes. "Good luck," I mouth.

Daniel scoops her up in a big hug. "Where are we going, princess?"

"McDonalds!"

Daniel groans. "What about a place that has yummy spaghetti? You love spaghetti! Or pizza? Or how about tacos?"

Maddy taps her chin. She loves having this power. As she considers her options, Jaxon comes down the stairs, shoes in hand. "Jaxon come too, Daddy!"

Daniel looks at me and then him. He bends down and picks Jaxon up in his other arm. "I'm sorry, buddy, tonight is Maddy's special night."

"When Jaxon night?" he asks, big crocodile tears slipping down his cheeks.

"Oh, buddy!" Daniel hugs him and kisses the top of his head.

"No, Dad! It's my night. No one else had to share! He can't come! That's not fair!"

"Hey, Maddy, calm down. I didn't say he was coming."

Jaxon's crying grows louder. "Jaxon come too! Jaxon night!"

Daniel looks to me. I step over and pry Jaxon from his dad's arms. "I'm sorry, buddy, maybe another time," I say. "Tonight is Maddy's turn."

Jaxon points to himself. "No, Jaxon turn!"

"You better go," I say, shoeing them out the door while Jaxon begins to howl.

"So what did you decide?" Daniel asks as they step onto the porch.

"McDonalds!"

Daniel sighs and I smile to myself as I return to the kitchen. Jaxon continues to cry on my hip while I stir the sauce and add pasta to the boiling water. He cries on the stool beside me while I roll out the breadsticks and sprinkle them with parmesan cheese. He normally loves to help me cook. I thought giving him his special stool and letting him roll out dough would make him forget all about Daniel and Maddy.

Jaxon is still whimpering and occasionally muttering, "Jaxon nigh," even after dinner is over and he sits in the tub. He barely touched his food, even though pasta is normally his favorite meal.

I'm reading him stories in bed when the front door opens. Jaxon jumps up and dashes for his door. He slides on his stomach all the way down the stairs and attaches himself to Daniel's leg. "Jaxon night!" he wails. The tears start all over again.

"Buddy, it's bedtime," I say.

Daniel picks him up so Jaxon's head rests on his broad shoulder. "What do I do?" he asks quietly. I shrug. Daniel rubs our toddler's back and tries to soothe him. "You want some special Daddy/Jaxon time, buddy?"

Jaxon rubs his red, watery eyes and nods. Daniel looks at me. I shrug. "It's not like he has to be up early for school," I say.

"Okay, buddy, do you want some ice cream?" he asks.

Jaxon's entire face ignites with joy. "Ice cream!"

Daniel goes back out the front door. "We'll be back in an hour," he says.

I take Maddy upstairs while she excitedly regales me and Addy with the details from her special night out. I help the girls bathe and get ready for bed before reading stories and tucking both girls in. Then I poke my head into Olivia's room. She's ready for bed, snuggled under her covers and reading a book. "Lights out in ten minutes," I say. "You need to get back on your school schedule."

"Jaxon isn't even home yet. I'm not going to bed before a two-year-old."

"Fair enough. But go to bed as soon as you hear Dad get back. Okay?"

"Fine."

I close Olivia's door and walk across the hall to Danny's room. I tap on the door before poking my head in. His lights are already out. "Good night, buddy, I love you."

Danny starts pretending to snore. I know it's fake but I'm not going to push it. I close his door just as I hear the front door open. I walk downstairs to find Daniel holding our sleeping son in his arms. "He fell asleep on the drive home."

I smile at Jaxon's chocolate covered face. He's grinning in his sleep. "Did he have fun?"

"He had a ball. I took him back to the play place for a little while, and then we each got a chocolate milkshake. I have now been to that place three times in 24 hours. I think I've filled my quota for a year."

"You're a good dad." The words slip out without much thought. But Daniel smiles in a way I haven't seen in a long time. His eyes get misty. "Thank you," he says.

I take Jaxon from his arms and carefully start up the stairs. "Good night," I whisper.

"Good night. See you tomorrow. I love you."

My hands shake as I attempt to run the mascara brush through my strawberry eyelashes. I can't actually remember the last time I wore makeup. I used to love dressing up and putting makeup on in the mornings. I always wanted to look my nicest for Daniel. It's hard to look nice when you feel so disgusting. My occasional bursts of emotion are becoming less frequent but still happen often enough that makeup seemed like a waste of time. I'm beginning to wonder if I'm wasting my time right now, since my hand doesn't seem to want to cooperate.

I don't know why I can't keep my nerves in check tonight. I feel like I'm getting ready for a blind date or something, with how fast my heart is racing. I've been married to this man for fifteen years! We've been on hundreds of dates, so why am I freaking out? I guess I'm still not sure how to talk to him. Everything has changed so much between us. What used to be familiar and comfortable is now awkward.

I finish my makeup quickly, using a Q-tip to clean up the raccoon eyes I seem to have created. I put on one of Daniel's favorite tops. He says it makes my eyes pop. Then I run a brush through my short hair one final time. I'm actually making an effort tonight, which feels weird. At first I just wanted to wear my sweats, have greasy hair and not bother with makeup. I'm still mad. The little devil-shoulder part of me wanted to show up looking absolutely disgusting, just to stick it to him. I want him to know what he's done to me, and that I'm still angry. But after I thought about it for a while, I decided to take a shower and dress nicely. I may be angry and hurt, but I don't need to be immature. And he made such an effort to connect with the kids this week, it seems only fair I should do the same.

I herd the children into our blue minivan with complaints only from Danny, and start the trek toward Melissa's house. The kids start fighting like a pack of hungry hyenas the moment we pull out of the garage, but I barely notice. Tonight, my thoughts are louder. I still don't know what we're going to talk about or what I should even say to him. Before I can come to any sort of answer, we're here. The kids hop out and run for Melissa's front door. I unbuckle a squirming Jaxon and set him on the driveway. He takes off after the rest of them. I slide the back door closed and turn. Marge is standing directly behind me.

"When are you going to let that poor boy come home?" she asks. Her eyes are narrow and accusing.

"Not now, Marge."

"Haven't you made him suffer long enough?"

I clench my fists and try not to look at her.

"MOM!" Melissa comes running across the lawn and grabs her mother by the arm. "The kids want to show you what they're doing. Come inside and help me," she says, dragging her away. "I'm so sorry," she mouths over Marge's head.

Marge continues to glare at me. Her thin mouth turns up at the corners and I follow her gaze to Daniel. He approaches me with a bouquet of tulips, my favorite flower. I accept the gift and try to smile. "Thank you."

"You're welcome. Thank you for being willing to go out with me tonight."

I turn and wave to Melissa, who is standing in her open doorway, and then follow Daniel to his car. I set my flowers on the backseat and climb in through the door Daniel is holding open. "Thanks."

"You're welcome." He gives me a nervous smile. We're being very polite. Maybe that's why I feel so uncomfortable. Daniel closes the door behind me and goes around the car to climb in the driver's side.

"Thanks for taking Jaxon out last night. He really had a good time. All the kids did."

"My pleasure. You look stunning tonight, by the way. I really love that shirt on you. The green makes your eyes shine."

"Thanks." I try and fight it, but my cheeks blush anyway. "So, what's the plan tonight?"

"I'm taking you to Sullivan's."

My favorite. I'm glad now that I decided to get a little dressed up. Daniel has the wheel gripped tightly in both hands. His knuckles look white. For as long as we were dating, and ever since, Daniel has always driven with one hand and held my hand in his other. This must be a weird adjustment for him. As it is, I'm sitting on my own hands in case he slips into old habits. We make small talk as we drive. I have so much I want to say and yet no words will come.

We pull up to the restaurant entrance, where my door is opened by a handsome young man in a tux. He flashes me an award-winning smile. Before, I would have found him charming. Now all I can think when I look at men is whether or not he's an addict too.

I always thought addicts were disgusting, greasy-haired men with yellow teeth, beer guts, and still living in their parents' basement. Going to group and my experiences with Daniel have shown me anyone can be an addict. My entire perception of men has changed.

Daniel hands our keys over to the valet and we walk inside. The host asks if we have a reservation and Daniel gives him our name. He then guides us straight back to a table. I'm actually impressed. Daniel really planned this out.

Once we are sitting, Daniel asks if he can move to the same side of the table as me. My heart races, but I tell him it's okay. The bench is small, so our arms touch when he sits down. I can feel the heat from his body radiating toward me. "I'm sorry," Daniel says. "But I want to be able to talk to you, and I don't want others to overhear us. You know, it's kind of a sensitive topic."

I nod my understanding. "What is it you want to say to me?" I ask. It's strange having him sit so close to me. I can smell his cologne taking over my nostrils. The advantage to his being so near is I don't actually have to look him in the face while we talk.

Daniel takes a deep breath. "Here goes. I don't think I will ever fully understand the pain I have put you through. For that, I am so, so sorry. I love you more than anything in the world. I wish I could take back my stupid choices, but I can't. What I can do is become better for our future. I understand you need your space. Take all the time you need. But I do want to be a family again. I will spend the rest of my life trying to fix what I have broken. And I will do whatever it takes for you to trust me and feel safe with me again. I really hope that someday you will be able to forgive me."

I knew I shouldn't have worn makeup. My eyes water, but no tears flow. I want to believe him. More than anything in the world, I want to believe him. But he lied to me for fifteen years. My heart is screaming to take him back, but my head is waging a battle of its own. "How do I know you won't just slip back into old habits again?"

Daniel sighs deeply. "I know you don't trust me yet. And I know I can't guarantee I will never slip up again. This addiction is powerful. I can guarantee you I will try every minute of every day to stay sober and regain your trust. Whatever it takes and no matter how long it takes. I won't give up, if you don't give up on me. I finally understand now that this is an addiction. For years I convinced myself that it was just a bad habit that I could stop at any time. Ryan has helped me see that this is an addiction and I cannot overcome it on my own. It will take years to retrain my brain and find healthy outlets for stress, like meditation and exercise. But I am going to fight to reach that goal."

I stare at Daniel. I can't help it. I've never heard my husband admit to any sort of weakness before. He's always believed himself to be superman. "How'd you get so humble?" I ask.

I continue to watch his face and I can swear he actually blushes a little. "Well, Ryan has helped a lot, but I've also been going to a 12-step program every week. Sometimes multiple times a week. Step one is to admit that I'm powerless to overcome my addiction and that my life has become unmanageable. Until reading the words in that first step, I didn't understand how true they really were. I was living a lie and I hated it. I felt like I was living two lives. It was exhausting. I was filled with so much self-loathing and anger, and I know I took it out on you and the kids. I am so grateful you caught me when you did. I'm afraid of where my addiction could have gone if I had continued."

The waitress comes over to introduce herself. Her presence alerts me back to reality. I was so lost in Daniel's words, I had almost forgotten we were in a restaurant. I look up and immediately cringe. The waitress's blouse is split almost to her naval, revealing just how blessed she is. My toes curl and I shift away from her, causing the leather bench to groan. How are we supposed to battle this addiction when pornography is everywhere? Especially when it's bent over, pouring our water. I order quickly and glance at Daniel, wondering if he will allow his eyes to linger.

Daniel stares down at his menu while he rattles off his order, and then hands the menu to our waitress without looking up. I continue to watch Daniel. He realizes she is gone and looks up slowly. "Sorry," he mumbles. I squeeze his arm.

"You did great," I whisper.

Daniel closes his eyes and I begin to wonder if he's okay. A minute later he opens them and glances at me. He looks away quickly and clears his throat. "I... uh... I've been talking to God."

I almost drop the glass which is halfway to my lips. "Seriously?" I laugh. When I realize Daniel isn't joking, I set my glass down and look at him again with widened eyes. I'm not sure who this imposter is, but he's certainly not the man I married.

"The second step in the program is about believing in a higher power who can restore you to physical and mental health. I know it sounds crazy, Sarah, but I found God. I started praying and I think he's listening. For once in my life, I feel hopeful about our situation."

I sit back in my chair and stare over at Daniel. My mind can't even comprehend what he is saying to me. I'm not sure how to react. Silently, I wave my hand forward, giving him the go-ahead to pray. Daniel bows his head and begins to whisper. I look around, hoping no one notices. I really hope our waitress takes a long time to come back. I can't hear everything he says, but I do catch something about him asking for strength in times of temptation. He silently ends and looks up at me again. I try and smile, but the disappointment behind Daniel's eyes make me think it didn't come across as very genuine.

Daniel clears his throat. "I'm on step three right now. It's about turning your will and your life over to God."

I nod slowly. I feel like that's all I've been doing tonight. I finally find my voice. "I didn't know you even believed in God."

"I didn't either," Daniel says, taking a long drink from his ice water. "I guess I always assumed he was there. I don't think we're just on this earth by some coincidence. I always hoped there was a purpose to this life, and a place to go after we're done living it, but I never really sat down and established what I believe."

"Until now?"

"The program gave me the courage I needed to really find out for myself if there is a God. He gives me strength when I'm feeling weak. Without Him, I had no hope for me. I had no hope for us."

"Why didn't you tell me about all this?" I feel blindsided. "Why didn't you tell me you were in a 12-step program, and about the whole God thing?"

Daniel stares hard at the small vase of flowers in the middle of our table. "I was embarrassed," he whispers. "And I didn't know what your reaction would be."

I take another sip of water. A different waitress comes over to our table and brings us our drinks and salads. She explains how our first waitress went home for the night and she would be taking over. This waitress is cute, but her shirt barely swoops below her neck. I look at Daniel. He just smiles.

Chapter Nine

*D*ear Sarah,
It's time to forgive your husband. If not for him, for yourself. You need to find peace. You cannot do this while you are holding on to anger and hurt. Turn to the Lord. He will take the pain for you. In fact, he already did.
Sincerely, a friend

I close my phone and chuck it back in my purse. I'm in a nice restaurant filled with people, otherwise I would be screaming and swearing by now. I pick up my wine glass and immediately put it down again. I'm afraid I'll crush the glass. I don't know who this person is, but they are getting more and more bold. I sit back against the firm booth, too stunned and angry to speak as I wait for Daniel to return from the bathroom. Forgive him? Just like that? And where is all this Jesus talk coming from? I've never been a religious person in my life. First my husband, now this "friend" want me to find God. Unless... the thought hits me like a cold bucket of ice, dripping down my neck. My body breaks out in chills and I move to the edge of my seat, anticipating Daniel's return.

He smiles at me from across the restaurant, as he makes his way back to our table. I look at him through narrowed eyes. His smile fades into concern when he sees my face. He sits carefully and leans forward. "Is something wrong?"

"Have you been e-mailing me?" I accuse, pointing a finger in his direction.

"What?"

"I don't need you to play dumb. I need the truth. Have you been sending me e-mails since I kicked you out and signing them as being from a friend?"

Daniel stares at me blankly. "No," he says slowly. "Someone is e-mailing you... about us?"

"Yes! Since the morning after you left. I get an e-mail almost daily. The return address is weird and if I try and reply to ask who it is, I get a delivery failure notification."

Daniel watches me for a few moments, his face unreadable.

"I'm not making this up!" I say, louder than intended.

"I believe you. I just can't imagine who or why..." Daniel's voice fades off. "What do these e-mails say?"

I pull my phone out and open the newest message. I hold it up for him to see, with a shaky hand, and then watch his face closely for clues. His eyes scan over the message quickly. He genuinely looks surprised.

"I would never push you into forgiving me," he says, lowering his eyes. "I mean, I hope you do someday. But I'm not setting a timeline."

"So it's really not from you?"

"No, I'm sorry," he says, shaking his head.

I look at the e-mail once again before putting my phone away. "Who else have you told? Who has known about this since the beginning?"

"The only person I've told is Melissa. I've talked to her and I talk to the guys in my 12-step group, but that's it, I swear!" Daniel's eyes and voice indicate he's telling the truth. In addict mode, he would have become defensive and angry at my questions. The sincerity and humbleness he has shown me tonight speak volumes. He hasn't acted out in a while. I can see the difference now.

"What about Melissa?" I ask. "You don't think—"

"No, I really don't think she would be that bold or forward," Daniel says.

I raise my eyebrows. "Your sister?"

Daniel smiles. "She wouldn't be that bold to you. To me, she has said plenty, trust me. But she knows how much you're hurting. She wouldn't do anything to hurt you more or push you."

I frown.

"I will ask her tonight, though, if it will make you feel better."

I sigh and shrug my shoulders. The waitress comes over and sets our food in front of us. It looks and smells incredible, but I'm suddenly not as hungry anymore. I poke at my perfectly cooked steak and a tiny trickle of blood runs into my baked potato.

"I'll ask Melissa," Daniel says, offering me a hopeful smile.

I nod and slice into my thick, juicy steak. I stab a piece with my fork and begin nibbling on the corner. I frown down at the chunk of delectable meat. This is my favorite food in the entire world. I wish I felt hungry enough to enjoy it.

Daniel clears his throat. "So... uh... what do you think about what this e-mail friend said?" he asks. His eyes dart around the restaurant, looking for anywhere to land except on me.

As I swallow a small bite of buttery potato, the skin flakes against my tongue. "You mean about forgiving you?"

Daniel coughs nervously. "No, I mean about the whole Jesus atoning for our sins part."

I ponder his question carefully. I fork three green beans and bring them to my lips. Normally I don't like restaurant vegetables. They're always overcooked and mushy. I place the beans in my mouth and crunch into them. These ones are the perfect combination of soft and crispy. Finally, I look at Daniel until he has no choice but to return my gaze. "I honestly don't know," I say. "I've never really focused on religion. I just wasn't raised that way. But in listening to you talk, I guess I feel similarly. I want to believe in an afterlife. I don't believe that when we die, that's it, we're just gone. As far as praying to God and having complete faith in him to take away this pain, I'm just not sure if I can do that."

Daniel bends over like I've just knocked the air out of him. He looks down at his plate. That was clearly not what he was hoping to hear.

"But I'll certainly give it some more thought now," I add. I glance down at my plate. It doesn't look like I've touched my food.

Daniel notices my round eyes and his forehead crinkles. "Aren't you hungry?"

"I honestly don't remember the last time I ate a full meal," I admit. Since the separation, I just haven't had an appetite at all. I ask for a to-go box and hope I have more appetite later.

Daniel pays the check and as we're leaving the restaurant, he asks if I want to go for a walk with him.

"Do we have time?" I ask.

"Yeah, I pushed our appointment back with Ryan. I told him I wanted to take you on a date first."

"Then sure," I say, though I'm not certain my twisting stomach will agree.

The sun is all but gone, leaving just a hint of pink above the horizon. A group of grey clouds move in overhead, threatening to burst. We used to spend a lot of time in the city before the kids were born. Now we hardly ever come downtown. Walking down the street with sparkling city lights on either side, reaching up toward the sky, almost feels magical. I look up and close my eyes. Daniel walks up behind me and stops. I can feel his warm breath again my neck. It causes my arms to break out in goosebumps.

"Race you to the ferris wheel!" I yell, breaking my hand away from Daniel's and dashing ahead of him. My thighs burn from exertion, yet I watch helplessly as Daniel passes me. I pretend to stumble and moan, clutching my ankle. Daniel slows down and glances back. He bends over me, his eyes soft with concern. "Are you okay?"

I grin wickedly, shoving him so he falls over and speed ahead. I can hear Daniel laughing behind me. "Oh, I'm going to get you for that!"

I scream eagerly, but I don't slow down. I reach the end of the line and stop, panting. I turn. "I win!" Daniel charges straight for me.

"No, no, no!" I squeal, putting my hands out.

Daniel barrels his broad shoulder into my abdomen and scoops me onto his shoulder. "You're such a cheater!" he says, placing my kicking legs back on the ground.

I laugh and reach up, warming my frozen fingertips on his cheeks. He flinches against the cold, smiling.

"But that's one of the things you love about me," I say.

"You know I do." Daniel wraps his arms around my waist and pulls me against him. I shift up to my tiptoes to meet his lips. My hands slide up the back of his neck and into his thick, wavy hair.

"Oh, get a room!"

Daniel and I pull apart to see Kelly standing in line behind us. Even though we're not in high school anymore, I can still feel the hatred pouring from her eyes as they burn into me.

"Oh, hi Kelly," Daniel says politely. He steps behind me, wrapping his hands around my waist and rests his chin on the top of my head.

Kelly huffs and drags her friends away.

I try not to laugh, but I can't help it. Being a cheerleader and homecoming queen, she always felt entitled to Daniel's affection since he was the quarterback of our football team. Some unwritten rule somewhere said they were apparently meant to be together. Unfortunately for her, he preferred the short, sporty red-head from the girls' soccer team. We were clearly a crime against humanity, or at least high school.

Daniel pulls me forward and we climb into the bright yellow gondola. I slide across the seat and Daniel sidles up right beside me. He puts his arm around my shoulders and kisses my hair while the ride operator warns us not to stand up in a bored voice. With a lurch, we begin to rise. We climb higher and higher, the metal creaking and squeaking beneath us. I look across the dark sky and stare at the sparkling city lights below us. A breeze blows across my face, filling my lungs with the salty sea air. Daniel brushes a warm hand across my face, turning my cheek to face him. He kisses me gently, sending tingles up my spine. Four years together and he still has the ability to make my toes curl.

We go around once, but as we're nearing the top for a second time, the gondola lurches suddenly and we stop. Daniel and I both put our hands out to catch ourselves from slamming into the metal lap bar. We stare down at the bottom of the ride. People crawl along the base of the ferris wheel, like ants, but nothing seems to be happening.

We sit for several minutes. Daniel's eyes begin darting anxiously around. "No, no, no," he mumbles.

"It's okay, babe," I say, rubbing his thigh. "I'm sure they're just loading more people and we'll start to move in a minute."

The bored operator gets on a megaphone and shouts up to us. We can't make out everything he says, but we catch enough to understand.

"Ride...Broken...fix...wait...fire department."

"Did he say fire department?" I ask excitedly, leaning forward. "Cool."

Daniel's face goes white and his legs begin to bounce anxiously. "Not tonight," he mumbles. "This can't be happening."

"Relax, sweetie," I say, grabbing Daniel's hand in mine. I rest my head on his shoulder and snuggle into his warmth. "Let's just sit back and enjoy the gorgeous view."

Daniel shakes his head and tries to stand. I grab his arm and pull him back down. "What are you doing?" I shriek. "Why are you acting so weird? I know you're not scared of heights."

Daniel looks at me and lets out an exasperated sigh. Then he scoots to the edge of the gondola and points below. "Do you see those lights down there in the shape of a heart?"

I glance in the direction he's pointing and squint. "Yeah, I can see them," I say. I look back at Daniel and shrug my shoulders. "So?"

"Those are candles," he explains. "In the center of those candles is a little table and two chairs. By now, sitting on the table is a warm, delicious meal from Sullivan's. There's flowers, and cheesecake, and both our parents, just waiting.

By the time we get down from here, the food will be cold, the candles will be burned up or blown out, and everyone will be gone." He puts his face in his hands and leans over the bar. "It was supposed to be the perfect proposal," he whispers.

My jaw drops open. I stare at Daniel. He sits back and smiles. Reaching into his shirt pocket, he pulls out a small black box and opens it. A beautiful, sparkling diamond winks back at me. "Sarah, this isn't how I wanted to do this. You have the most perfect setting for a proposal waiting below, yet here we are, stuck fifty feet in the air. I can't wait another moment. I can't waste one more day without asking you to be mine. I love you, Sarah! And I want to spend the rest of my life loving you. Will you marry me?"

My hand flies to my open mouth. Tears prick the corners of my eyes. "Yes!" I shout, throwing myself against his chest. "Absolutely, yes!"

Daniel stands behind me, staring up at the city lights. We have so much history together here, I can't imagine living anywhere else.

"Can I... ?" Daniel starts and then stops.

I turn to face him. "Can you what?"

He shakes his head. "Never mind." He wrings his hands together and walks more quickly.

"What?" I ask, grabbing his arm and stopping him mid-stride. I look up into his face.

Daniel squeezes his eyes shut. "Can I hold your hand?" he asks. He peeks one eye open to gauge my reaction.

I pause briefly. "Okay," I say. Daniel lets out a breath of air and intertwines his fingers with mine. We've been holding hands for years, yet this feels like the first time all over again. His hand is warm in mine and it sends tingles up my arm. We walk hand in hand up and down the street, admiring the beautiful lights and busy sounds of the city. My heart flutters as I realize how much I'm aching for the man walking beside me. In moments like this, I wish we could just go back to the way things used to be. I open my mouth to tell him I don't want to be separated anymore, but a sinking feeling in the pit of my stomach stops me in my tracks. I close my mouth and listen as he continues to tell me about work. I know the timing isn't right. My gut is telling me he's not ready yet to come home.

We dash from the car to Ryan's office building and still end up completely soaked. The angry grey clouds from earlier tonight finally followed through on their threat. I try to ring out my dripping hair with little success. I glance over and laugh at Daniel, who looks like he's trying to shake off like a wet dog. I catch myself and stop. I don't remember the last time I laughed like that. It feels good to laugh, and yet it feels forbidden. Like, under the circumstances, I'm not allowed to be happy, if even for a moment.

Daniel flashes me his most charming smile and then he reaches for my hand as we run up the stairs together. When we walk in his office ten minutes late, laughing and dripping wet. Ryan greets us with a broad smile.

"Well, I take it the date went well?" he asks.

"It did," I respond. We sit on the couch side by side. I allow Daniel to hold my hand again.

"Would you like to discuss the possibility of Daniel moving back home?" Ryan asks.

My body immediately tenses. I can tell Daniel feels it too by the way his jaw tightens. "I'm just not sure," I hesitate.

"I don't mean today, or tomorrow even, but it's important to set up some boundaries and possibly some stipulations for Daniel's return so he can know what to work for."

I relax a little, but my back remains rigid and on guard. "Okay, like what?" I ask.

"Well, it's up to you. What worries you about having Daniel come home?"

"I don't want pornography in my house ever again."

"Okay, so can the two of you think of some ways to prevent that?"

"We need a good filter," Daniel says.

"I don't like that his computer is downstairs, in the dark basement, where he can be all alone."

"Daniel, can you agree to move your computer upstairs, to an area where it can be more closely monitored?"

Daniel sighs deeply. "I guess. I mean, I know that would help with the temptation to relapse. But working upstairs will be so much harder with all the kids coming in and out."

"Okay," Ryan says, nodding. "But won't it be worth it to have your kids back in your life every day? And if it gives Sarah peace of mind… "

Daniel puts his hands up in defense. "Okay," he says. "I know you're right. And with the constant threat of a child walking into the room, that will definitely help with my temptations."

"And that is how you do it," Ryan says, clasping his hands together. "You just created one boundary for your home to help you both feel safer."

I have the distinct impression a weight has been lifted from my shoulders. This really is a good idea. "I also want a big picture of our family right next to the computer, so he can remember what we're fighting for."

"Absolutely," Daniel agrees.

I glance at Daniel and begin biting my thumbnail. I'm not sure how to bring up the next one.

"Sarah?" Ryan says my name. I look up at him guiltily. "You look like you have something else you'd like to say."

"I… ummm…" I glance back and forth between my husband and our therapist. "I don't think Daniel should have internet on his smart phone," I finally blurt out.

"What?" Daniel shouts. He turns his body to face mine. "But I use my phone for work and school almost every single day," he says, his voice tight.

"And you used it for porn almost every single day," I whisper. "You told me your cell phone was how you accessed it most of the time." I begin wringing the life out of the pillow in my hands.

"So you want me to delete my web browser?"

I nod slowly, worry filling my mind. What if this is it? What if this is the deal breaker and he leaves me here, just like Joe left Breanna? Ryan's eyes dart between the two of us, but he doesn't jump in or say a word. He just sits back and observes.

Daniel closes his eyes. I watch his chest rise and fall with each calculated breath. Daniel pulls his smart phone out of his pocket, pushes a few buttons, and hands it to me. "I deleted my web browser, my ability to install new apps, all my social media, and YouTube. Is there anything else?"

I stare at his phone, stunned. "And you're okay with this?"

"I don't want to be sick anymore. And I really, really want to come home. I need you to put in a new password, one I can't guess, and then if I need to install anything new, I have to come to you first. If I can't get to it, then I won't be tempted anymore. Out of sight, out of mind theory, right?" He tries to make a joke, but his voice is strained.

A small grin creeps across my face. I begin typing in the new password. Then I remember his worry and pause. "Wait. What about work? You said you use your web browser all the time to look up things for work.

His face falls. "Oh yeah."

"Can I make a suggestion?" Ryan asks. "I love seeing the two of you working together, by the way. There are web browsers you can get on your phone that don't allow explicit content. If you delete your current browser and install one of those, you should still be able to look up work related things—phone numbers for businesses, addresses, and that sort of thing without allowing explicit content, articles, or images."

I smile. "Thanks, Ryan, that's great!"

"What do we do... um..." Daniel grunts. "What happens if I come home and I do manage to relapse?" He stares at the floor, clearly not wanting to ask the difficult questions.

I look at Ryan. "People at my support group were talking about relapses last week. Are they common?"

Ryan looks between the two of us. "There is always the risk of a relapse with an addict. Yes, they can happen, and yes, unfortunately they are common. But let's get one thing straight. I've heard people say relapses are just part of recovery. This is not true." He looks Daniel square in the eyes. "Relapses are part of addiction. They are not part of recovery."

Daniel nods and swallows loudly. "I understand."

"But," Ryan says, "and this is a big, hairy but."

We both smile at his attempt at humor.

"A relapse is not an excuse to fall into a pit of self-pity again. If you ever do slip up, don't let it diminish the progress you've made in recovery. Keep moving forward and stay strong." Ryan turns and faces me. "We often like to use the 24 hour rule around here, but the two of you are welcome to establish whatever consequences make you feel safe."

"And what's the 24 hour rule?" I ask.

"If Daniel has a relapse either with viewing a form of pornography, masturbating, or both, he has 24 hours to tell you about it. If he does not, and you find out after 24 hours, the consequence is stricter."

I turn my head and look at Daniel. "What do you think? What would be a good consequence?"

"If I tell you within 24 hours, I have to sleep at Melissa's house for the night. If you find out after 24 hours, I have to move out for a week."

I look at Ryan. "That seems fair."

"Okay," Ryan claps his hands together. He shifts in his seat and tucks one leg beneath him. He wiggles around like an excited little puppy. "You are making huge jumps in your progress today. The last thing I would suggest is having a check-in every night. It's a great habit to be in, for any couple really. It gives insight into your partner and helps build a jumping point for open communication."

"What's check-in?" Daniel asks.

"You establish a time every night or every day to check-in with each other. There are five parts to it," Ryan says, holding out his hand. He touches each finger as he goes through the steps with us. "You find out how the other person is doing physically, emotionally, spiritually, sexually, and then how many days your partner has been sober. Would you like to try it?" he asks.

Daniel and I look at each other.

"Right now?" I ask.

"Yes," Ryan nods. "Go ahead." He points to Daniel. "Ask your wife how she's doing physically."

This seems weird. Daniel obliges and turns to me and asks, "How are you doing physically?"

"I'm fine," I say.

We both look at Ryan, whose shaking his head. "One of the rules is that you need to think of real answers. Fine and good are not answers. Those are cop outs. Now, you're trying to establish open communication with your husband again. Give him a real answer, so the two of you can begin connecting."

I look at Daniel and laugh nervously. This feels so silly. "Okay, I have had a headache for most of the day. I haven't been able to sleep well lately and I don't have much of an appetite. I feel tired all the time. It makes taking care of the kids tough. I'm more ornery when I'm tired."

"Good!" Ryan encourages us to continue.

"So how are you physically?" I ask.

"I've been working out every morning to curb my cravings. That makes me feel really good. I struggled with eating and sleeping for a little while too, but the exercise has helped."

"So maybe I need to start working out?" I ask.

"Good! You are both doing great!" Ryan's enthusiasm makes me smile. "Do you feel that connection you're making now? Check-in can open up so many conversations between a couple. Please continue."

"Okay, how are you emotionally?" I ask.

"I miss you, and I miss the kids. I'm sad I don't get to see them off on their first day of school. I miss the funny things the twins say around the dinner table. I miss kicking a soccer ball or tossing a football outside with Danny after work. I miss Olivia's hugs. I miss Jaxon's energy and watching them all grow and complete every day accomplishments. I miss lying in bed and talking with you until it gets so late, we giggle like little kids. I miss waking up with you by my side and the way you would burrow into the covers like it's a cocoon. I miss your soft, sleepy kiss each morning before I leave for work."

Daniel's blue eyes bore into me as he speaks. They cloud over with mist, and he wipes as them with the back of his hand.

"I hate myself for ruining so many good relationships. But I've been doing my meditations and I've been working on learning to love myself. I'm hopeful I can prove to you how sincere I am in my recovery and come home someday, when you're ready."

Daniel is playing my heart strings like a well-worn instrument. A nagging thought keeps me from giving in. "You keep saying when I'm ready," I cut in. "But it's not just about me. You need to be ready, too." My voice is calm but firm. "You were home with us for fifteen years and you could never kick this addiction. Look at how much stronger you're getting right now by being away. It wasn't until you were faced with losing everything that you started to truly change."

"This is good," Ryan whispers.

"You're right," Daniel says. "I don't know how long I would have kept down that self-destructive path if you hadn't found me. I tried changing on my own, but it never worked. I am so grateful you caught me that day! And I'm grateful for this chance."

"*Kintsugi*," Ryan whispers.

I tear my own eyes away from Daniel's sapphire ones. "What?" I ask Ryan. Daniel turns and looks at him, waiting for an explanation.

"Sorry," Ryan says. "Would you like to continue with doing check in?"

"No, now you have me curious," I say.

"All right. Check-in can take a long time, hours even, when you haven't been communicating regularly for a long time. But I want you to work on doing check-in every night. Call after the kids are in bed or something. Okay?"

We both nod. I'm actually surprised at how quickly one simple question opened the door and helped us talk genuinely with each other. I've been struggling with knowing how to talk to Daniel lately. I think this will help us a lot.

"You are creating *Kintsugi* right now, and I love it!" He's so excited that it's hard not to feel eager, though I have no idea why. "*Kintsugi* is a Japanese art form. When something precious breaks, like a dish or a bowl, they don't throw away the broken pieces. They don't even glue the bowl back together because the glue will make the bowl weak and it will be unusable. They fuse the bowl or dish back together by pouring gold into the cracks. When the gold dries, the bowl is more beautiful and even stronger than it was before.

"This is how I view your relationship. You have been broken, shattered even, by a crushing blow. Instead of throwing away something that is precious to you both, and instead of gluing the pieces back together or trying to pretend like the blow never happened, you're working to make it stronger than ever. Your cracks are there. Every mistake you've made is visible. You are filling those cracks with gold and making them stronger and more beautiful than ever. *Kintsugi*."

Chapter Ten

I find myself looking forward to Wednesday night. I honestly didn't think I would want to go back, but I have so many questions and I don't know where else I can ask them. After what feels like the longest last two days of summer in the history of summers, Wednesday arrives. I wake to an alarm for the first time in several months. My bones creak as I roll out of the blanket cocoon I've made for myself. I never thought I'd feel this old at thirty-five. I think about exercising more as I stumble down the hallway. I tap lightly on Danny's door before pushing it open. I see a mound of covers and think how much he is like me. I crack his blinds so the rising sunlight peeks into his room. Nothing. I sit on the edge of his bed and gently shake him awake. Nothing. I get meaner and peel the covers off his body, throwing them back. He rolls over and groans.

"Come on, Danny, get up. First day of school!" I try to sound chipper but, even to me, it just comes across as loud and annoying.

"Go way. I'm tired," he mumbles.

"Come on, sweetie, aren't you excited to see your friends? Third grade will be awesome!"

He mumbles something again and tries to reach his covers off the foot of the bed. I gently slap back his hand.

"Danny! Get up now!" The sweetness is gone from my voice. I mean it, and he knows it. Danny grumbles as he rolls off the bed and makes his way down the hall to the bathroom.

I roll my eyes, trying not to feel overly frustrated. After all, he's his mama's boy. I'm feeling much more awake as I enter Olivia's room. She is dressed, her hair is brushed, and she's sitting on the edge of her bed tying her new pink sneakers.

"You know school doesn't start for another hour," I say.

"I know, but I'm meeting Gentry and Eliza there early so we can swing before school starts. There's always a big line for the swings, so we never get a turn. Besides, if you hog one, the recess monitor will make you get off. And they're not very nice about it."

I smile. "Sounds like you have a fun morning planned. What can I get you for breakfast?"

Olivia looks at me like I just slapped her across the face. "Mom, it's the first day of school."

"Of course," I say, backing out of her room. My stomach drops. Daniel always makes his famous blueberry banana pancakes on the first day of school. It's been our tradition since Olivia's first day of preschool.

I make my way down to the twins' room and first shake Addy, who is asleep on the top bunk. Then I bend down and tickle Maddy in the bottom bunk. "Come on, my big girls, first day of kindergarten!" They both peek at me through slitted eyes. Then Maddy jumps up. "First day of school? Can I wear my new dress?"

"Of course, sweetie."

"Yay!" she giggles with excitement.

As soon as Addy realizes her sister is up, she sits up and scrambles down her ladder. "I want to wear my dress, too!"

"Matching! Matching!" Maddy sings, pulling the bright purple dress over her head. "Are our pancakes ready Mommy?"

I sigh again. I can't get out of it. I give the girls a weak smile. "You finish getting dressed and then come in for breakfast, okay? We'll do your hair after."

The girls cheer and scramble to pull on their sparkling zebra stripe leggings. I close their door quietly, hoping Jaxon will sleep a few minutes longer. I'm going to need a head start. I don't even think I have a recipe for Daniel's pancakes. He's always been the one to make them. I rub my eyes and step down the final two stairs. Turning the corner, I walk into our kitchen and smell fresh pancakes. I look around, thinking Olivia has decided to be ambitious and get started without me. There is no one in sight. Then I see a plate on the counter. I lift the tall pan lid and find a stack of beautiful, golden pancakes. They're still warm. There are no dishes on the counter or in the sink. I look around again. A small note rests beneath the magical pancake plate:

I hope you don't mind, but I snuck into the house before work. I didn't want to disappoint the kids on their first day. Love, Daniel.

I read the note four times before tucking it back underneath the plate. My eyes begin to water. I wipe them on my long pajama sleeve and pull out another pan. I begin cracking eggs into a bowl. I'm just whisking a little milk into the mixture when Olivia comes in. She sits on one of the barstools and looks at me expectantly. I pull a plate down out of the cupboard and remove the lid from the pancakes.

"Help yourself."

Olivia eyes me skeptically before gingerly lifting one off the plate. She holds it up to her nose and sniffs. "Are they the same as Dad's?"

I roll my eyes and pour eggs into the pan. It sizzles as I stir them around. "These are Dad's pancakes. He made them this morning before work."

"Dad came home?" she asks, her face brightening. She drops her pancake onto her plate and reaches for a fork.

"No, not quite." I kick myself for the poor choice of words. "He just stopped by to make you guys breakfast."

Olivia's face falls, pulling my heart down with it. She pours syrup all over her pancake and begins to eat silently. I finish scrambling the eggs just as the twins walk in. They both sit at the table. "Yummy, pancakes!"

I put a small pancake and some eggs on each of their plates. I scoop some egg onto Olivia's plate. She eats quickly and then grabs her backpack and waves goodbye. I glance at the clock. Where is Danny?

"Eat quickly. I'm going upstairs to find your brother," I say, turning to the twins.

"He's sleeping," Maddy says.

I hurry up the stairs and find a sleepy-eyed Jaxon coming down. He's clutching his blue monster blankie in his hands. As soon as he sees me, he reaches his arms up to be held. I scoop him up and carry him into Danny's room. Sure enough, he has crawled back into bed, the covers tucked under his chin.

"Daniel Linus Dunkin, get up!"

He jumps into the air and lands on his floor with a thump. "Ow!" he says, getting to his feet and rubbing his bottom.

"If you don't get dressed and downstairs now, you will not have time for breakfast. Now scoot!"

Danny pulls open a drawer on his dresser and begins plopping clothes on the floor.

I head back downstairs and sit Jaxon in his booster seat. Danny decides to make an appearance with only five minutes to spare. He grabs the last pancake from the plate and drops it again. "It's cold."

"Not my fault," I say. I finish putting the girls' hair in pigtails and tell them to grab backpacks. Danny complains as he puts the cold pancake in his mouth and forces down a bite. I grab Jaxon from his seat and herd the kids out the door.

When we get to the school, I realize I'm still in my pajamas, and I haven't even brushed my hair yet. I must look like a zombie apocalypse survivor. And it's the first day, so I have to walk them in. I groan and begin unbuckling kids. I try not to make eye contact with anyone as I scramble to get the twins to their classroom. Danny waves when we pass the third grade hall.

"Wait, don't you want me to walk you in?" I ask.

Danny eyes me up and down, and scoffs before he turns to walk to class.

"Bye! I love you, have a good day!" I shout. I smile when his shoulders slouch in response. The payback is satisfying. He pulls on his backpack straps and, ducking his head, continues down the hall. I shift Jaxon to my other hip and move quickly toward kindergarten.

After kisses and hugs, the girls eagerly bounce into their classroom. I make my way back out of the school as quickly as possible.

The house feels quiet with everyone gone. I get Jaxon dressed, put on a movie, and climb in the shower. At last. The hot water pricks at my back. For reasons I don't understand, I begin to cry. I'm so confused. I cry tears of joy for Daniel's thoughtfulness with the kids this morning. I cry tears of frustration over Danny. What happened to my sweet boy? I cry tears of sadness over Daniel. I don't want to be angry anymore, but every time I think about the life we lost because of his selfishness, the hot tears begin flowing again. My brain can't let those things go. My thoughts circle over and over again. All the what-ifs. All the missed opportunities.

The garage door slams, causing my heart to jump into my throat. I wipe my hands on the red and white striped towel and walk toward the sound of heavy footsteps.

"Daniel?"

His face is stony, his eyes red. "I lost my job today," he grumbles, dropping his bag on the floor. I put my arms around him, but he quickly pulls away. Turning, he punches the wall behind him, leaving a dent.

"Daniel! I know you're upset, but we'll figure this out. Did they give you a reason? Was it cutbacks?"

"Low performance issues," he shrugs.

I open my mouth to ask another question, but he stomps over to the couch and throws himself into it. I follow him. "What do they mean, low performance issues? If you were doing something wrong, shouldn't they have warned you first?"

"I don't know! Get off my back, okay? It's hard enough without you asking so many questions."

Olivia steps timidly into the living room, rubbing her eyes. "Daddy," she says with a smile. Her little toddler legs move quickly across the floor, and she settles into his lap. I can hear Danny crying in his crib upstairs.

"Great, the kids are awake from their naps early." I sigh and shake my head. "So what does this mean?" I ask.

"It means I don't have a job and we don't have any income," he snaps.

"So what about Disneyland? We've been planning this trip for months."

Daniel rubs his hands through his hair. "I guess we can't go now."

"Disneyland?" Olivia whimpers.

"Maybe next year," Daniel says. Olivia begins to cry. Daniel sets her on the couch and stands.

"I can't deal with this right now." Daniel retreats to the basement, leaving me with two crying kids and the aching feeling of being punched in the gut.

I slow my breathing and focus on the air moving in and out of my lungs, the way Ryan taught me to. I think about therapy. Focusing on the bad moments keeps me locked in the past. I can't move forward in my marriage unless I'm concentrating on the good, the person Daniel is becoming. I close my eyes again and return to the memory.

With Olivia on one hip, I climb the stairs and push the door open to Danny's room. His tiny body kicks erratically as he screams for food. I set Olivia down, handing her a basket of board books to look through and scoop Danny into my arms. I settle into the rocking chair and begin nursing him. Daniel appears in the doorway a moment later.

"I'm sorry," he says, his head hanging. "It's been a rough day, but I shouldn't have taken it out on you."

He settles on the floor beside Olivia and pulls her onto his lap. They read stories while I nurse the baby. When he's done eating, Danny begins to scream loudly. Nothing seems to soothe his colic. I bounce and rock him. I feel like I haven't slept in days.

"Here," Daniel says, getting to his feet and reaching for our son. He begins singing softly and paces around the room. Danny settles into his shoulder and is soon sleeping again.

"It's not fair," I whisper. "It's like you have magic hands. He never does that for me."

Daniel smiles. "It's a gift," he whispers back, winking at me. "Why don't you go take a nap? You look exhausted."

"Really?" I ask.

He nods. "Olivia and I can go watch a movie. You get some rest while this little guy is being calm." He sets Danny back in his crib and shoos us both out the door.

I kiss him softly. "Thank you."

I sigh happily, my tears gone. I lean into the now tepid water. I hear a tiny tap on the door. "Mommy?"

I shut off the water and step out. Opening the door, I'm met by his huge brown eyes. "What's up, buddy?"

"My movie over."

"What?" I step in front of the mirror. My body is raw and pink from the steam and heat of the water. My hands are shriveled and wrinkly. I glance at the small black clock, hanging over the toilet. Sure enough, almost an hour and a half has passed.

❤ ❤ ❤

I walk into group with more enthusiasm tonight. I'm anxious, but not as nervous this time. The familiar room is set up exactly the same as last time. Three women already have chairs pulled close together and are chatting when I enter. I'm surprised when one of them looks up and says, "Hi, Sarah."

I take a step back and she laughs lightly. "I'm not stalking you. I just remember your name from last time." She offers me a warm smile and pats the chair beside her. I sit and the other two women stop talking and turn to me.

"How are you doing?" one of them asks.

"Fine," I say, giving the socially acceptable answer.

She looks into my eyes and I swear she can see through me. She actually seems to want to know. She's not just asking to be polite. I squirm a little in my seat. Although I told myself I wanted to ask a question tonight, I don't feel ready. They're all looking at me expectantly. I take a deep breath.

"I'm doing better than last week. It's hard. I want to heal and move on with my life, but I don't know what to do. I don't know if I should forgive my husband and let him come home, or if I should be done with him and us as a couple. I just don't understand why this has to be happening to me." I look up at the ceiling, hoping they won't notice my eyes are no longer dry. When I look back down, the women are all still watching me. None of them have the pitying look I expect to see. They all look at me with… understanding. I feel relieved.

"As much as you hate to hear this, it really just takes time. Every day things, like eating and sleeping, will get easier."

"Follow your heart," another lady says. "If your husband is really making an effort to get better, he might just be worth sticking with. I'm on my third marriage." She smiles when my mouth drops open. I'm guessing we're the same age. "Every one of my husbands has had this addiction in one form or another. The first time, he wanted to work through it, but I didn't. I played the victim card and said I'd find someone better. When this secret came out with my second husband, I was more mature and in a better place to work through things. We did for a little while, and then he decided he didn't want to give up his porn habits and his prostitutes. He left me to live the way he wanted to live. My current husband and I have both been working hard at recovery. I realized I was still holding onto bitter feelings from my first two marriages. Our therapist has really helped me work through my issues.

"I'm not trying to tell you what to do," she says, putting her hands up. "I just want to share my story with you, so you can decide for yourself. I see a lot of women turn their backs on their husbands because they're hurt. And rightfully so! But in my case and many other women's cases, if you trade in your addict, you'll most likely end up with another addict of some form or another. If you have a partner, like my husband now, who wants to be a partner, who genuinely wants to get better and is willing to put the work in, why would you not stick by them? Through sickness and in health, right? I believe now that addiction is a form of sickness. I didn't sign on just to leave when things get tough."

I nod my head. I've never really thought about it like that before. I've been so focused on me, I haven't given a ton of thought to the contract Daniel and I made with each other when we got married.

The third woman pipes up, "Don't mind Angie," she says. "She is a veteran to the program and is very passionate about her views. Every situation is different and you need to decide what's best for you personally, and for your family as a whole."

As I look at these three women, their beautiful faces seem to shine. I want to be like them. I want to feel happy and peaceful again. And I want to be able to talk about these things without crying or feeling sick to my stomach. I clear my throat and ask the question that's been on my mind since Daniel took me out to dinner. "How did you guys find peace through this? How did you forgive your husbands?"

They exchange looks but it's the one who said hi to me when I first came in who speaks. "Pray. I don't know if you're a religious person. I didn't use to be, but now I am. I prayed to my father in heaven and He helped me through it. I had to be willing to work at it too, though. A prayer isn't like saying a secret incantation. The problem won't magically go away. You won't suddenly feel happy and not angry anymore, but having Him on my side and knowing He's got my back has helped immensely."

The other two both seem to agree with her. "We're not all the same religion or believe the same things, but we do all know there is a loving God who can give us strength if we simply ask."

Breanna sits next to me and lets out a big breath. "Sorry I'm late," she says, panting. "Work was insane today. I just got off and had to race to get here."

The mediator stands and welcomes everyone. I look around and realize the room has been filling up while we were lost in conversation. When the open discussion starts, the conversation quickly turns to forgiveness. I look around at all these women, all different ages, races, and circumstances as I sit back in awe. It's amazing how we can relate to each other on this level, even if we can't in any other way. I listen to many women share their stories of God, or Buddha, or whoever they pray to and how that higher power has brought them strength and comfort. How they couldn't have found forgiveness without His help. Before long, I realize the discussion is being wrapped up and I never said a word. I'm enjoying hearing from all of them so much, I don't feel like I have anything of value to add.

Sharing begins and I listen carefully to each of the women as they share their name and their personal stories. One woman in particular catches my eye. She is tiny and has the biggest, roundest belly I've ever seen. She looks like she's ten months pregnant. I look at her in admiration, especially when she speaks. She had to have gotten pregnant very shortly after finding out about her husband's addiction. I'm not sharing my house with my husband right now—I can't even fathom sharing a bed with him.

We were talking about having another baby not too long ago. I know people would have called me crazy. People think five is too many, but I love being a mother. I truly feel it's my calling in life. I thought I could balance a large family until my husband went and screwed everything up. It seems like the discussion about adding to our family took place years ago now, but it wasn't much later when I found out about Daniel and kicked him out. Now I wonder if I'll ever get another baby. This woman gives me hope.

The next lady begins talking about her boyfriend and how he relapsed during the week. My heart aches for this complete stranger. She starts to choke up when the women on either side hold her by the hands. She clears her throat and continues. "I'm so tired of all my friends telling me pornography is not that big a deal. That all men look at it, all men masturbate, that it's just what men do. I just want to shake them until they understand. Remember when cigarettes were cool and the commercials all showed famous, beautiful people with them? Now the cigarette commercials feature a man with no legs or a woman with a hole in her neck telling everyone how dangerous it is to smoke. Society still acts like porn is cool and normal. When will they catch up to the facts about how dangerous and addictive it is? When do we get our commercials with the twisted bastard who lost his wife, family, and job to porn?" It's probably inappropriate, but the room erupts into applause. She smiles, showing off her cute dimples and sits down.

When it gets to my turn I grit my teeth and stand. My knees begin to shake, I reach a hand back and grasp my chair so I won't fall over. "My name is Sarah."

"Hi, Sarah."

I smile. It was annoying and weird last week. This week I find it endearing. "I've been married to my husband for fifteen years. We've known each other for as long as I can remember. We dated all through high school. We went to college together and got married when we were twenty. I thought I knew my husband backward and forward, inside and out. All my friends were jealous of our strong relationship." My voice cracks and I can feel Bre reach up and grip my hand. She squeezes slightly, giving me the strength to continue.

"The bond and communication we had was incomparable to anyone else I knew. When we were talking about marriage, he informed me that he had struggled with pornography off and on as a teenager. I too was naïve and thought it was completely normal for a teenage boy to do that sort of thing. I shrugged it off. I mean, I know I'm not perfect either. I made mistakes in my younger years, too. Teenagers make mistakes. It's what we do. I knew for certain it wouldn't be a problem anymore. Why would he look at smut when he has the real thing right here?" I gesture to myself.

"We have had five kids together in the last fifteen years. Things have never been easy for us, but I thought our life was good. My husband went to school part-time, trying to finish his degree while working full time. I never understood why he struggled so much with school. He kept failing classes and had to retake them. A four-year degree took him almost ten years to accomplish. He's been let go due to performance issues from three jobs. We have five kids, but we struggled to get each one of them here. We even got checked and were told my husband's sperm count was low. Then the last year or so, we've been fighting more. My husband would lose his temper really easily, and over the stupidest things. There were times I had to ask him to leave the house until he calmed down. I could never put my finger on why we seemed to be struggling so much. Then about a month ago I went down to my husband's office and caught him… "

My breath shudders as the memory gets caught in my throat. Breanna gives my fingers a squeeze and I feel an unfamiliar hand slip into my open palm. I look down at the lady on my other side. She gives me an encouraging smile.

"I will never be able to forget that disgusting image on his computer screen. I couldn't believe it! My husband was cheating on me with an electronic device. He begged for forgiveness and cried about how sorry he was. It didn't take long to find out he has been struggling since we got married. He confessed that he's never gone more than a month without viewing porn in our entire marriage. Most recently, it's been even more often, until he's been seeking it daily. That is fifteen years filled with nothing but lies. Suddenly everything made sense and I felt like a complete idiot for not figuring it out sooner. This is why he struggled in school. He chose porn over homework. He's lost three jobs because of his addiction. He was becoming more angry and bitter and easily frustrated because he was living two lives. He was getting tired of trying to hide his secret. He was stressed out all the time. His relationship with me and the kids was changing. He pulled back a lot. He preferred to be alone rather than being with other people, even his own friends and family.

"We've been going to a great therapist who is trying to help us work through everything. It's just so hard, though! Some days I want to pretend nothing ever happened, bring my husband home, and move on with our lives. Other days I'm so mad, I'm ready to call a divorce lawyer and just be done with him. I feel like walking away would be so much easier than this hell he is putting us through. Then he does things like sneak back home to make pancakes for our kids' first day of school this morning and I'm reminded of why I'm still here.

"I was diagnosed with a form of PTSD, which has been hard to wrap my head around. On the one hand, it's made me not feel quite so crazy. Therapy has been great for both of us. For the first time since he was a teenager, my husband has started to feel hope. He was lost in this addiction. I feel like I'm finally getting to find out who the real man is that I married, and it's beautiful to watch. I was terrified to come here the first time and talk to strangers. I don't feel like you're strangers anymore. You're all my soul mates. You understand me. I love having a safe place to come, so thank you."

I sit down and glance around the room nervously. Everyone is looking at me and smiling or nodding. A few are wiping their eyes. I take a deep breath and look at Breanna for her turn. As she looks back at me, the lights catching on her tears, making her eyes sparkle.

Chapter Eleven

*D*ear Sarah,

I'm so proud of the progress you are making! I can see your countenance beginning to change. You and Daniel both seem to be improving each day and are beginning to heal. It's beautiful to watch! But you are still missing one very important step. It is essential that you find a way to forgive your husband. Even if you decide to walk away from this marriage, you must first forgive. Otherwise you will waste your life in bitterness and misery.

Sincerely, a friend

I smash my fists into the keyboard. The computer screen goes blue and then black. How dare this "friend" tell me when I should and should not forgive the man who spent fifteen years deceiving me? I am trying desperately to keep my head above water when I feel like all I'm doing is drowning in worry and sorrow. I get to decide when I'm ready, not this... person. This is not the kind of friend I want to have any more! I vow to never open another e-mail message from them again. I don't care if they've been right so far. I unclench my fists and try to slow my heaving breaths. My cheeks flash with heat and I want to do more than break the stupid computer. I take to kick the foot of my computer chair, but now my foot throbs in pain along with my head. I hear Olivia's sweet voice outside my bedroom door.

"Mom, are you okay in there? I heard you yell."

I thought that was in my head. "Yeah, sweetie, I'm fine." I focus on calming my breaths to hide the tremor in my voice. I walk into the master bathroom and turn on the cold water. Leaning forward, I splash the icy liquid on my face. It stings the heat in my cheeks, but I feel myself calming down. I need to be composed before I leave this room and start getting kids ready for school, or I know I will lose all patience with them. It's not fair to them how messed up this addiction has made me. I know I'm not the calm, patient, loving mother I was a few months ago, when I thought my life was great.

I splash my face again and slip from the room, hoping to make it downstairs unnoticed. As I mix muffins for breakfast, I start to feel semi-normal again. I'm not sure how much longer I can handle these crazy emotions and mood swings. I thought pregnancy was bad, but it's got nothing on PTSD.

The kids begin clambering down the stairs, ready for food. I sniff once and look up, ready to greet them. "Good morning!" I say in my cheeriest voice. "Muffins will be ready in about fifteen minutes." Almost immediately the twins begin fighting about who gets the biggest one. My little mini-me tries to break up their fight.

"It doesn't matter. They all taste the same," Olivia says.

"You're not the mom!" Addy yells at her.

"Yeah, stop being so bossy!" Maddy kicks Olivia in the shin and runs.

"Madison! Get back here!"

Olivia chases her little sister and pins her to the ground, sitting on her chest. Addy runs around them, trying to knock Olivia over while Maddy screams bloody murder.

I move away from the kitchen to rescue and scold Maddy, but just as I do the timer beeps. I yell at the girls to knock it off while I throw open the oven door. I reach in, not thinking, and burn my hand on the hot muffin pan. "Ow!" I shout and run for the sink, running my sizzling fingers under cold water. Danny comes downstairs and begins yelling at me that the house is too loud and Dad would never have let them get away with this. He then tackles Olivia and my living room turns into a full blown WWF ring. Jaxon begins crying upstairs—I'm sure he's terrified his house is under attack. What an awful way to wake up.

The oven continues to beep, adding to the chaos and the noise. I slam the water off and use my left hand to awkwardly remove the now crispier-than-intended muffins. I turn the timer off and, with my throbbing hand, rip my two oldest apart. They both look disheveled and messy.

"Get it the car!" I yell through gritted teeth, my eyes flaming. The twins both begin to cry. "SHUT UP!"

I yell even louder. "JUST SHUT UP AND GET IN THE CAR!" My voice breaks as my terrified children rush into the garage. I follow them, handing everyone a half-burnt muffin, and begin backing out of the garage. My minivan is filled with the sounds of sniffles and angry mutters. I suddenly slam on the breaks, causing muffins to fly through the air and fall to the floor. I swear under my breath and lay my head on the steering wheel. Amid wails about dirty breakfast I dash from the car and run inside. I grab a sobbing Jaxon off the kitchen floor and run to put him in his car seat.

I pull up to the school and watch as the kids all climb out. They have messy hair and wrinkled clothes, clutching their mostly burned muffins, grumbling and whining while they walk inside the school. As I drive away again, I wonder how long it will take before social services ends up on my doorstep. Jaxon continues to cry until I get him home and hand him a muffin and his orange juice. I settle him on the couch, pajamas and all, and turn on a movie. I hate that the stupid box has become his babysitter lately, but if I don't go upstairs for a moment of peace, my brain might just explode.

I open my bedroom door and fall face first onto the comforter of my unmade bed. My hands, especially the fingertips, sting like crazy. I look down at the white blisters beginning to bubble up on the skin and begin to whimper. "Ow."

I hear my phone ding, alerting me to a new e-mail. I pick up my phone and glance at who it's from. Sure enough, it's from my special friend. I close my phone and throw it across the room. Daniel's words run through my mind. Breanna and the voices of the other ladies from group echo his words. The e-mails flash through my thoughts as well and I finally give up, crumpling to the floor. I have no idea what I'm doing. This is very new to me. I'm not even sure I know how to pray. I don't know what to ask for either. I just know I can't keep doing this. I'm out of strength physically, mentally, and emotionally. I'm drained and I need help.

I get off the floor and, feeling rather stupid, pick up my phone which is thankfully not cracked. I open Google and type in "how to pray." I skim through about a dozen different answers before deciding prayer shouldn't be this confusing. I close my phone again and kneel beside my bed. I clasp my hands together as I close my eyes. "God?" I pause, realize quickly he's not going to answer, and continue. "I'm sure you don't know me. I'm pretty insignificant in the grand scheme of things, but I'm here. And I need help. I don't know what to do about my marriage. I don't know how to forgive. And I'm out of energy. I'm not sure how much more I can take. Please, God, if you're there, please help me. Please give me strength." A lump begins to rise in my throat. "And please help me not feel so alone."

I sit back on my feet and wait. Tingles begin forming on my arms and work their way up to my neck, where the hair stands on end. A warm feeling swells inside me, so overpowering I can't open my eyes. I continue to sit, my heart swelling so much that I can't help but smile. Tears prick the corners of my eyes. I let out a breath of calm. I feel warm and good and happy all over. Almost as quickly as the feeling comes, it fades and is gone.

I open my eyes slowly and look around, half expecting to see a heavenly messenger in my bedroom. I try to stand, but my head swims and I have to sit back down. I get up more slowly this time, still lightheaded. I go downstairs and snuggle up close to my baby. He rests his blond little head against my chest as we watch the remainder of the movie together. I smile to myself and kiss his sweet, soft cheek. God is indeed real, and he loves me.

The next week seems to fly by. Soon fall will be upon us and the real rainy season will begin. It seems as though there is a constant drizzle outside all day, every day. Maybe a month ago this would have bummed me out. Today, as I drive the kids to school, I only see how beautiful the tree-lined streets are from all the rain.

I drop Jaxon off at Melissa's house straight after dropping the other kids at school. Our therapy appointment with Ryan is earlier today due to some meetings he has this afternoon. I actually find myself looking forward to it as I drive down the street. I hum along with the happy song on the radio. No one wants to hear me sing, not even myself. I park the car and climb up the steps to the building. Daniel and Ryan are already inside when I arrive. They are both leaning forward and speaking very quietly, so I tap on the door to announce my arrival. They both jump back from each other and look at me, almost guiltily.

"Am I interrupting?" I ask.

"No, not at all," Ryan says, getting to his feet. He gestures for me to sit down and then closes his office door behind me. "We didn't want to close the door so you would feel welcome walking in, but we didn't want anyone to overhear our conversation either." Ryan looks to Daniel to confirm. Daniel looks at me quickly, and then his eyes dart away. Something is up.

"So what were you talking about then?" I ask. I notice Daniel is sitting a little further away from me today. When he doesn't reach for my hand I pick up the fringed pillow, my old friend, and begin playing with the tassels.

"Daniel has requested, and I feel it's a good idea, to hold a formal disclosure."

I look at Daniel, who doesn't return my gaze. He fidgets nervously with his fingers. I turn my gaze to Ryan. "I've heard women at group mention it, but I'm not sure I understand exactly what a formal disclosure is."

"Well, right now Daniel is finishing up step four in his 12-step program, which is to write a searching and fearless moral inventory of himself. Step five is to share this list with himself, God, and at least one other person. Daniel wants to share his list with you. He says you are his closest friend and he doesn't want there to be any secrets between you anymore. He wants to share everything he has done and everything he has been through with you. A full disclosure means exactly what it sounds like. He wants to disclose everything he has done, while lost in this addiction, to you. The formal part of it means I will be there as well. I will formally act as the mediator for this meeting. Do you feel like you are emotionally prepared and could handle doing a formal disclosure? I need to warn you, they are not easy. But Daniel feels, and I agree, that this could be the last step to getting him home again. Many couples who are struggling need to go through a formal disclosure before they can make a decision about whether or not to stay together. But, like I said, they aren't easy. A lot of wives are able to forgive and move on without knowing all the nitty-gritty details."

"Should he be confessing to me though?" I ask. "Shouldn't it be like to a priest or someone?"

"Daniel feels strongly that he wants it to be with you. But he understands if you don't want to, or feel like you can't handle knowing everything."

I look at Daniel. When he still doesn't return my gaze, I place my hand on his arm and pull him towards me. His head turns and I can see how red his beautiful eyes are. "Why aren't you talking to me?" I ask. "I feel weird that Ryan is speaking for you, even though you're right here."

"Because I'm scared," Daniel says, looking at his shoes. A tear runs down the bridge of his round nose. He quickly wipes it away with the back of his hand.

I hold his arm tighter and lean into him so my head rests against his broad frame. Ryan continues to explain the details of the full disclosure.

"First of all, it is recommended that you drive separately. You need time to process alone after having everything disclosed. It is also recommended that you leave a window of 24 hours after a formal disclosure before talking to each other. Again, this is for your safety and to give you time to process. It would also be a good idea to have a good friend or family member you trust that you can turn to after disclosure for emotional support. Daniel is almost done with writing out his inventory. He and I will go through it together and determine what needs to be disclosed. Then the three of us can meet in a safe place and hold the disclosure together." Ryan locks his fingers together and rests his elbows on the desk. He leans forward. "What are your thoughts?"

I take a deep breath. "Okay," I say, nodding. "I think I'm ready."

"When do you think would be a good time to meet?" he asks, looking at Daniel. "Does next week work for you?"

Daniel nods. "Yes," he croaks, and then clears his throat. "Yes, I think next week would work well, and that will give me enough time to be prepared."

"Does that work for you, Sarah?" Ryan asks.

"Yeah," I shrug.

"Where would you like to have the formal disclosure? I recommend some place quiet and comfortable. Nowhere public, like a restaurant."

"Can't we just come here, to your office?" I ask.

Ryan places a hand over his heart. "Oh, Sarah, I'm touched you find my office comfortable." He shoots me a cheesy grin. I return his smile.

"Here works for me, too," Daniel says. "We've gotten comfortable talking here."

"Okay, let's plan for next Friday then, here in my office at 5:00?"

"Can we make it 5:30?" Daniel asks. "That way I won't have to leave work early."

Ryan looks at me. I nod. "As long as Melissa can watch the kids that night, then it works for me, too."

"Good! Now that we've got that settled, how is check-in going?"

"Really well," I say. "I'm glad you taught us how to do that. I feel like we're really starting to connect again." I laugh. "Last night our conversation lasted almost two hours."

Ryan's grin splits his face. "That's amazing, and exactly what I like to hear."

"I'm really struggling, though, with talking about how I'm doing sexually." My eyes dart over to Daniel and back at Ryan. "I don't know what to say right now, you know, with all the betrayal trauma. Talking about anything sexual gives me really bad anxiety." Now I'm the one looking down at my hands.

Ryan leans forward. "There's no shame in how you feel. Remember, shame fuels this addiction. If you don't feel comfortable talking about your sexuality yet, then take it off the table for a time. Just make sure you establish a day when you will talk about it again. That way it's not gone indefinitely and you can both prepare yourselves to discuss it when ready."

Daniel smiles at me weakly. "How long do you want to take it off the table?"

"Why don't we skip it until November 1st?" I ask. "That will give us a month." I secretly hope Daniel will be home and I'll be more comfortable by then.

We leave Ryan's office together. "Do you want to grab some lunch?" I ask.

"I wish I could," Daniel sighs, "but I need to get back to work."

"Oh, okay." I turn to walk toward my car.

"Sarah," he stops me with his voice. "I'm sorry I was so distant today. I've been really focusing on my list lately and it's making me depressed. And I'm really, really scared of what's going to happen to us after the final disclosure. I'm not trying to withdraw, and I'm still sober," he reassures me.

I smile inwardly. I love seeing the therapy have an effect on him. He never would have said something like this to me any other time in our marriage. "Thank you for telling me. Your distance made me a little nervous today."

"I love you, Sarah."

"Bye, Daniel."

Stacy Lynn Carroll

Chapter Twelve

After several days and at least three un-opened e-mails, when my phone chimes, I decide to open it this time. I sigh before tapping on my e-mail icon. I skim over the messages of hope and encouragement and look at the newest e-mail.

Dear Sarah,
Don't give up your hopes and dreams for the future.
Don't put your life on hold because of this addiction.
Sincerely, a friend

I know exactly what they are referring to. My mind has been on babies a lot lately. As Jaxon gets older, I can't let this idea of another baby go. But I'm terrified! What if things don't work out with Daniel? What if he decides sobriety is too hard and he leaves me, like Breanna's husband? I'm not sure I want to bring another child into this mess. I'm also afraid if I wait too long, it won't happen. We've had a hard enough time getting pregnant. I don't want to add my aging body to the timeline. Now that Daniel is sober, maybe his sperm count won't be so low this time and we'll get pregnant easier….but in order to get pregnant, I would actually need to have sex with my husband. Right now I can't even talk about it without feeling anxious, and we haven't so much as kissed since he moved out.

I rub my throbbing temples. My thoughts are swirling inside, attacking me at every turn. I drop to my knees and pray for clarity. When I get up, a thought enters my mind and I know what I need to do.

Melissa's kids are sick, so my mom comes over to watch the children while Breanna and I go to group.

"It seems like you've been leaving your kids a lot lately," she says when I answer the door. "They are your first priority."

I clench my teeth. "Mom, if you can't babysit, just tell me. I can find someone else."

"No, I'm fine. I just wish you would tell me what is so important that you keep disappearing."

Before I can think of how to respond, Jaxon and Addy come running into the entryway. "Grandma!"

She bends down and catches them both in her outstretched arms. "Where's Daniel?" she asks over the kids' heads.

"Daddy has to live somewhere else for a little while until he gets all better," Addy explains.

My cheeks burn, but I don't want my mom to see, so I turn and pretend to look for my keys even though they're in my pocket.

"Grandma!" Maddy comes tearing into the room. Her socks slip on the hardwood and she falls. My mom rushes over to scoop her up. She tries to calm Maddy's sobs, but Maddy begins crying louder. "No, I want Mommy!"

I take her from my mom and sit on the couch with Maddy on my lap. I stroke her long red hair and whisper soothing words. My mom walks over and sits beside me. Jaxon crawls onto her lap. "See?" she whispers. "Your kids need you."

I know my mom means well, but her words sting me to the core. It takes every ounce of self-control I have not to fight or yell. I look at her over Maddy's head and try not to glare. "Mom, I have not been doing very well lately. And you know very well that Daniel is not living here right now. You're smart and I know you've figured that out. I'm not sure why you insist on my saying it out loud. These children are my number one priority. Everything I do is for them, including trying to get myself healthy again. I need your support right now, not your criticism."

There's a knock on the front door. Maddy jumps off my lap and races Addy to open it. I get to my feet and grab my purse. My mom stands with me and puts an arm around my shoulder. "I'm sorry," she says. "I love you and I'm worried about you. I am here for you if you need anything."

"Thank you." I can hear Breanna's laughter from the entryway as the girls attack her. "Bedtime is at 8:00 please. They have school in the morning."

"You got it," my mom nods.

Breanna and I get to the meeting early. I'm disappointed when we're the first ones there. I pour us each a cup of coffee, and we sit.

"How are you?" Breanna asks, nudging me with her foot. "I feel like we haven't talked in a while."

"I know. It's weird. Well, Daniel and I are getting ready to do a formal disclosure on Friday."

"Wow, good luck! Joe would never go for that. I think that's one of the reasons he ended up leaving. He refused to be that open and vulnerable with me. He liked his secrets and his lies too much. But I'm dating Bronson now, and things are going really well."

"Oh, yeah! Tell me about Bronson! I can't believe I've never even met this mystery man yet."

"Hopefully soon," she smiles. "If I don't scare him away with all my baggage first." She laughs and I join her.

"I'm sure he has plenty of his own. We all do!"

"Yeah, it's true. We had a long talk about pornography the other night. It's not something he has really struggled with, but he did open up to me about a problem with alcohol. He is three years sober, and has gone through the 12-step program. He also has a five-year-old daughter from his previous marriage, which ended because of his addiction."

"Wow," I say.

"I know, right?" Breanna's eyes light up when she talks about him. It's both exciting and adorable to see. "I'm just trading one addiction for another." She chuckles. "If I had met Bronson right after Joe left, I would have run for the hills. But the mere fact he's so open about his addiction and where he is in recovery, it all just makes me like him that much more."

Breanna continues to gush about her new boyfriend while my eyes travel to the open door. I feel like a stalker, waiting for one woman in particular to arrive. When she walks through the door, belly first, I jump to my feet.

"Okay, so I guess we're done talking now."

I look down at Bre. "What? Oh, I'm sorry! I just really want to talk to her," I say, pointing.

Breanna's lips begin to curl and I realize she is just teasing me. She gestures for me to go. I approach the tiny woman from behind as she's pouring herself a glass of ice water. "Excuse me," I say, tapping her shoulder, "Do you mind if I ask you a couple questions?"

She turns and smiles at me. "Not at all, but let's go sit first. My back is killing me." I follow her as she waddles over to the nearest seat. "I can't help but notice you're pregnant," I say.

She laughs and rubs her round belly. "What gave it away?"

"I'm wondering... gosh, I don't even know how to word it."

"You're wondering how I could be having another baby with an addict, especially one who has been sober for less than a year."

"Yes!" My response is more enthusiastic than I intended. "How are you doing it? Do you have other kids? Aren't you worried about all the what-ifs?"

She chuckles and I can't help but think I must seem crazy to her. "First of all, I had all your same fears. But what-ifs will always be there. What-ifs are a part of life, whether you're married to an addict or not. So discredit those worries right now."

"I guess you're right."

"I have two other kids at home. They are six and almost three. I knew I wanted one more so my husband and I began trying for a third. We had only been trying a few weeks when everything came out about his addiction. At first, we put the baby on hold. It made me so mad! He stopped our family in its tracks and I resented him for it. One night during group, I had the realization that if I end up divorced and a single mom to two kids, or to three kids, will it really make a difference?" She chuckles.

"I know it probably sounds weird and twisted to you, but I just reached that point. He was not making the decision for me. I was handing him the decision. So I took it back and told him we should keep going. He probably asked if I were sure a dozen times, but I told him yes. I wanted another baby and I didn't want to wait. My situation is completely abnormal. I'm just weird, I guess, but I've never regretted my decision. My husband relapsed about two months ago, but he's been doing well since then and we're doing well as a couple. You just need to follow your heart, and be in the right place mentally and emotionally to make a decision like that."

I lean forward and hug her. She is surprised but returns my embrace. "Thank you," I say. "You've really helped me a lot. I want another one too, but I've been too focused on the what-ifs. I haven't given a lot of thought to the what-if-I-don't question. If I don't, I will always wonder if my family is complete, and I will probably resent my husband forever for it."

She nods. "How many kids do you have?" she asks.

"I have five."

Her mouth drops open. "And you want more?"

I smile politely.

"Sorry," she says, shaking her head. "You are much braver than I am. Addiction or not, this is definitely it for us," she adds, rubbing her large belly.

I stand to return to Breanna.

"Good luck!"

"Thank you again! And I'm sorry, I forgot to ask your name?"

"I'm Suzanne," she says, "but you can call me Suzy."

"Thank you, Suzy. I'm Sarah."

I slip into my seat right as group begins. A few minutes into the discussion, a woman creaks the door open. Her eyes are wide and terrified, red and swollen from crying. She is in sweat pants and has a stain on her oversized T-shirt. She isn't wearing any makeup, and her greasy brown hair is pulled back into a loose ponytail. She plops into the seat beside me and folds her arms across her chest. I watch as her eyes dart anxiously around the room before landing in her lap.

We have a large group tonight, so the mediator ends the discussion early and turns the time over to sharing. Without thinking twice, I raise my hand. "I'll go first."

Bre pats my leg. I stand and look around. A lot of these faces are familiar to me now. I can even name at least five of the regulars in the group. The thought makes me smile.

"Hi, my name is Sarah."

"Hi, Sarah." The woman next to me jumps.

"My husband and I are having our formal disclosure on Friday. I know a lot of you have been in this position before. Thinking of you has given me the strength to go through with it. I'm nervous, but I'm also anxious for it to be over. I'm done focusing on everything he did. I want to focus on what he's doing now."

I sit down and Breanna stands to speak. When everyone says, "Hi, Breanna," the lady on my opposite side jumps again. I find my attention drawn to her more than anyone else who is sharing. She fidgets in her seat. Her arms keep going back and forth between folding them across her chest and biting her super-short nails. Each time a new woman stands to share, she appears jumpy and skittish. I just want to reach over and hug her. I can tell she's a first-timer. She's displaying all the signs I'm sure I exhibited my first night in group.

When the time comes for her turn, everyone glances in her direction. She looks up and stares, frozen, ahead. Her legs begin to tremble and her eyes dart between all our faces. I try and offer an encouraging smile, but she doesn't seem to really see anyone. She just stares ahead, like she's trapped and looking for a place to hide.

"You can pass if you want," I say.

Her eyes dart to mine and she nods. "Pass," she whispers before looking down at her fidgeting hands.

"Would you at least tell us your name please?" the mediator asks.

The woman jumps up out of her chair. "This was a mistake," she says and bolts from the room.

The mediator shakes her head, her sad eyes following the woman out the door. I stand and exit the room behind the first-timer. I find her around the corner, sitting with her knees to her chest, her arms hugging her legs. She rocks back and forth against the wall, crying. I sit beside her and don't utter a word. I understand all too well how difficult this journey can be. We sit side by side for several minutes, crying silently together.

When her trembling and her breathing seem to slow down, I scoot a couple inches closer and wrap an arm over her hunched shoulders. She tenses at first, but then her posture softens and she falls into me. With her head on my shoulder, she begins to sob. I continue to hold her without saying a word. Breanna finds us huddled on the floor together. She sits down on the hard cement on the lady's other side. She scoots closer and gently scratches the other woman's back. Breanna opens her mouth to speak but I shake my head. "Not yet," I mouth.

Several minutes later, she sits up and stretches both legs out in front of her. She wipes her eyes with the bottom of her T-shirt and tries to stand. Breanna helps her to her feet. I stand and give her a hug. "I'm Sarah," I say, "and I know this doesn't help right now, but I was exactly where you are only two months ago. Hang in there. And keep coming back here. It really does help."

"I feel so silly," she says. "I'm not sure if I can come back after my grand exit."

"Everyone here understands," Breanna adds. "No one in that room will judge you. Ever."

"Thank you both," she says, looking up at us through her long, dark eyelashes. "I'm Hailey."

"Welcome, Hailey," Breanna says. "I'm Breanna and I really hope we see you here next week."

Hailey nods and leaves quickly out the front door of the church.

"Do you think she'll be back?" I ask.

"Hard to tell," Breanna says. "Some people just aren't ready yet."

I look at the empty door she walked through and send a silent prayer heavenward for her.

When I walk in the front door, the house is quiet. I move past the stairs and into the living room where my mom is settled on the couch, reading a book. "Everyone seems to be asleep," I say, setting my purse down on the black leather.

My mom closes her book and turns toward me. "Oh, hi, I didn't hear the door." She gathers her book and reading glasses, pushing them into her bag. When she stands, her gaze meets mine. "I'm really sorry about earlier," she says. "I don't know the whole story, but I promise I will be more supportive." She pulls me in for a hug.

"I'm sorry I haven't told you everything but I just… can't."

My mom puts a hand up. "You don't need to." She walks toward the front door and pulls it open. "Have a good night, Sarah. Call me if you need anything."

I lock the door behind her and make my way up the stairs. I check on each of the kids before changing into pajamas and climbing into bed. My body is exhausted but my mind won't shut up. I pick up a book off my nightstand and begin to read. I've read more books in the last two months than I have in the two years previous.

My phone begins to ring and I glance at the clock on my nightstand. "Who on earth?" The red numbers blare 11:37. I pick up my phone to see that it's Daniel, and he wants to video chat.

"Hello?" I whisper, holding it up.

Even through the tiny, fuzzy screen I can tell Daniel is in a bad way. His face looks pale and clammy.

His normally blue eyes have dulled to a grey. And he's shaking violently. "Daniel, what's going on?" I sit straight up and climb out of bed to turn on more lights.

"I'm sorry it's so late," Daniel says, his voice echoing through our poor connection. "I just really needed to see you. I need to be reminded of what I'm fighting for." He attempts to smile, but it looks painful.

"What's going on?" I ask again. "Are you okay?"

"I am now," he says, sighing. "I'm just really struggling tonight. I had a really stressful day at work and the desire to act out is almost overpowering. I didn't know what else to do, Sarah. I kept trying to tell myself I need to stay clean for you and our family. I just can't get these thoughts out of my head." Daniel hunches over, holding his head between his hands. "I knew if I saw you it would help. And it has. You're beautiful, Sarah. You are the reason I'm battling this addiction." Daniel begins pacing the small room, his hands trembling as he runs them through his hair. All the motion makes me feel dizzy. I have to look away.

"Let's do check-in," I suggest. "Talk to me, Daniel. How are you physically?"

He looks into the phone. His lip starts to curve upward. "Really? Don't you need to get to sleep?"

"Not right now, I don't." I offer him an encouraging smile and try to distract his mind from the evil that's clutching it.

We talk until I fall asleep, the phone still clutched in my hand.

Chapter Thirteen

*D*ear Sarah,
No matter what happens during your formal disclosure, don't lose that hope you've been grasping so firmly. When times get hard and you don't feel like you can go on, drop to your knees and pray.
Sincerely, a friend

The day for my full disclosure with Daniel has arrived. I'm nervous with excited anticipation. I feel like this is the next step for us in having him come home. I'm not sure why he is so nervous to talk to me. I feel like I've already asked him a lot of the important questions about his addiction. There must be something else he hasn't told me yet, which scares me. I've been to my support group enough that I've heard countless stories of how this addiction has spiraled out of control. The addict always needs more to reach that initial high he felt. But he can never quite get there, so his addiction becomes more intense and often, more grotesque, in search of that fix. Their addiction shifts away from the "norm" to looking at things that used to disgust or shock them. Soon addicts are searching for images involving teens or children, or searching for same-sex, cross-dressing, bondage, or bestiality. Because they've built up such a high tolerance to arousing material, to feel excited many users have to combine sexual arousal with the feeling of aggressive release.

I already know Daniel has never looked at teen or child pornography, and he has never had inappropriate thoughts about teens or children. This was one of the first questions I asked him, back when I was filled with so much anger and sadness that I could barely sleep. I called him in the middle of the night once and he assured me he had only sought out adult women. I never would have let him near our children again if he struggled in that area.

My brain rushes over the other possibilities. I now know if an addiction goes long enough, untreated, the addict often will begin acting out with actual people instead of just images. This is when online dating, online or phone sex, lap dances, prostitutes, and affairs begin. I shiver thinking of all the possibilities. I know way more about this addiction now than I ever wanted to or thought I would. I find myself becoming more like the women in my group. I don't feel sick anymore when we talk about it. I can ask questions and speak openly without crying.

I close my eyes to block out all these negative thoughts. I try and change my focus to the other women in my support group. A lot of them have been through far worse than myself, and they are still happily married and going strong. No more focusing on the negative or the bad. It will only make me feel discouraged. Instead of worrying about the worst scenarios, I try and cling to that hope God has given me. I can do this. I can get through this.

Thankfully Melissa's family is well now so I don't have to rely on my mom again. I drop the kids off on Friday night, pausing to hug each one and tell them how much I love them. They each hug me back and return my 'I love you,' with the exception of Danny. Little Mr. Attitude merely grunts in my direction. I wasn't expecting this much insolence until my kids were teenagers. I blow him a kiss anyway and look to Melissa. "Thank you again. I'm not sure how long this will take," I say, biting my lower lip.

"Don't worry about it. I've got them. Go take care of you and Daniel."

The drive from Melissa's house to Ryan's office happens in a blink. I honestly don't even know how I got here. All I know is I'm suddenly pulling into the parking lot. I say a prayer for strength before climbing out of the car. I open and close my clammy hands, which are beginning to shake. I reach for the door handle and miss. I look up, grip the metal hold between my sweaty palms, and pull it open. I eye the staircase briefly before pushing the button on the elevator. I don't trust my nervous legs to get me up the stairs this time.

I enter Ryan's office almost at the same time as Daniel, who must have taken the stairs. He gives me a half grin, but the corners of his mouth turn down quickly again. "Hi," he says.

"Hi." I try and smile back, but my lips won't cooperate.

"Ladies first." Daniel gestures with his hand out so I step into Ryan's office. It feels darker than usual in here. That's when I notice the blinds are pulled tightly closed, I assume to offer us more privacy with this sensitive discussion. Ryan gets to his feet and offers us each a seat. Instead of side by side on his couch, like we normally sit, Ryan has two high-backed chairs facing each other in the center of the room. I sit so my body is facing the office door. Daniel sits opposite me and Ryan puts a sign on the door before closing it tight.

"Just as an extra precaution," he explains. "This is definitely not the type of thing we want to have interrupted. How are you both feeling today?" Ryan looks at me first.

"Nervous and anxious," I say.

Ryan looks at Daniel and he nods. "Nervous and anxious, and a little sick to my stomach. I haven't eaten all day."

Ryan sits behind his desk, which happens to be in the center of our two chairs. "I'm going to explain to you how this will go." He lifts a folder from his desk and references it as he describes what will happen.

"Daniel, you will read the timeline we created together to Sarah. Sarah, as hard as it may be for you, please wait until Daniel is finished before saying anything. After he is done, you may ask questions, and

Daniel has agreed and is obligated to answer them truthfully. Refrain from asking questions about details, like specific websites your husband has visited or the color of hair she had. Please understand that knowing details about your husband's sexual behavior will end up hurting you instead of helping. Details help us visualize our spouse participating in sexual behaviors with others. The more details we know about our spouse's experiences, the harder it will be for us to let go of the hurt and pain and move through the grieving process. Do you understand?"

"Yes."

Ryan continues. "Appropriate questions can be about suspicions you have had about your husband, how his addiction has impacted your relationship, how the addiction has impacted your family's finances, consequences of sexual behaviors that impact you, and any fears you have related to your husband's addiction."

"What do you mean by consequences of his behaviors that impact me?"

"Like if he had an affair with a prostitute, you can ask if he contracted an STD. That would definitely impact you."

My eyes widen. I stare down at my hands and begin twisting my wedding ring in circles around my finger. "And what types of fears can I address? Can you give me an example?"

"An example of a fear would be, did you ever touch our children inappropriately? Or did any of your sexual encounters happen in our home?"

I gulp. Maybe I'm not strong enough for this. "Okay," my voice shakes.

"Do you both understand the process?" Ryan asks.

"Yes."

"Yes."

"Okay then, let's get started." Ryan hands Daniel a piece of paper from the folder he has laid out on his desk. This is it. Daniel clears his throat. He holds the paper close to his eyes, not looking at me. I take a deep breath and close my own eyes. I'm not sure I can look at his face right now anyway.

Daniel lists a date and then his sexual behavior at that time. He begins with just years from his youth, other times he says specific months and year. This isn't so bad, I think. Then Daniel says an actual date which I recognize as being during our honeymoon. My eyes pop open in disbelief. I look up and see Daniel's fingers that grip the paper are shaking violently. I close my eyes and hang my head down. The next several dates go through our first couple years of marriage. I bring my hand to my mouth to keep any noises from coming out. I can't believe how often he sought porn. My mind is reeling with information. I'm glad I don't have that timeline in front of me. I think seeing the list of dates would actually make me sick.

Daniel says a date that makes my heart stop.

"Wait." I blurt the word out without thinking.

Ryan looks at me and shakes his head. I stare at Daniel, but he continues to read. My heart starts racing.

The lump in my throat grows so large, it hurts to swallow. I squeeze my eyes shut and shake my head. The dates keep coming. Each one slicing through me like a stab in the heart. Most of the dates don't mean much to me—they are just numbers. It's how often the numbers have the same month and year attached that have me panicking.

Daniel gets closer to the present and as he does so, my head begins to swim. I actually feel like I may pass out. I grip the edges of the seat and try to hold myself steady. He's about two years out now, shortly after Jaxon was born. His descriptions of acting out begin to escalate. He created a second, secret e-mail account. He got a subscription to a pornographic website. The free stuff wasn't enough anymore. He joined a dating website.

Wait, what?

My hand flies to my mouth again. My vision begins to blur. Now he's just a year ago. We're almost done. Please, God, tell me we're almost done. He says a date and I remember it well. Daniel was on a business trip last year and missed our twins' birthday party. Then Daniel says the words I dread most. The words I never wanted to hear and never thought I would. Last year, he slept with another woman.

I gasp. I look up at Daniel, my eyes wider than I knew was possible. I can see the tears streaming down his face as he reads. He closes his eyes and shakes his head. He sets the paper on his lap and places a hand over his eyes. His shoulders wrack with sobs. I look at

Ryan and see the moisture forming in his eyes as well. Neither of them look at me. I can't breathe. It feels as though someone has punched me in the gut and I can't seem to catch my breath. I choke on the tears that want to come, but can't. My body shakes from my hands to my feet. I begin to sway and worry for the second time that I might fall off the chair.

Ryan's voice comes out in a whisper, but cuts through the silence like a sharp blade. "Daniel, please continue."

"No." I shake my head violently. "I can't take anymore." I jump to my feet, still shaking. I rush past Daniel and race for the lobby, my vision blurring. I collapse into a chair. My head spins and I feel my stomach churning inside. Ryan cautiously walks up to the couch and sits on the edge beside me. He places a gentle hand on my shoulder.

"Sarah."

I continue to shake my cloudy head.

"Sarah," he tries again. "If you need to stop now, I completely understand." His voice is calm and steady. "But in my experience, coming back for a second time will only be harder."

I shrug off Ryan's comforting hand. He folds them in his lap and waits for a response.

"I don't think I'm strong enough," I whisper.

"I understand. I can tell you with absolute certainty that you are one of the strongest women I have ever met. Your recovery has been incredible to witness. Most women hold onto their anger and their hatred much longer. I've seen you demonstrate signs of love and forgiveness towards your husband already."

I snap my head up and look at him hard. "I have not forgiven that man," I hiss.

"I know. Forgiveness takes time. Trust takes even longer. But you are stronger than you give yourself credit for. I will be right there. Daniel is almost finished. Take a moment and come back when you're ready."

I silently offer up another prayer. I get to my feet and follow Ryan back into his office. I stare at the ceiling to avoid looking at my husband. I sit back in the chair and nod at Ryan. I don't have the strength to speak. He encourages Daniel to continue.

Daniel sniffs and holds his paper up again. He continues to read, but my mind doesn't register anymore. After what feels like hours of torture, he reaches the infamous date. Three months ago, when I caught him. I'm relieved to hear that is his final date on the timeline, but the relief is fleeting. It doesn't make up for the lengthy list of indiscretions before it.

Daniel sets the paper down and wipes his eyes. He glances at me, but only briefly. His face is red and spotty from crying. His jaw is clenched tight.

I let out an involuntary sigh. My mind tries to focus, to come back to the here and now, but I'm lost in dates and things my husband did that leave me terrified.

"Sarah." Ryan's voice is quiet, but it rings in my head. "Do you have any questions?"

I sit, frozen. My face burns and my body continues to shake. It takes all my focus to concentrate on breathing in and out. Questions. I know I had questions. Then one of the dates hits me like a sledgehammer. "Did you view porn the day Olivia was born?"

Daniel hangs his head. "Yes."

"Were we still at the hospital?"

"Yes. I was so stressed about being a dad that I went into the hospital restroom and..."

I put my hand up to stop him. "That's all I need to know." My stomach twists into knots. I can feel the bile rising in the back of my throat. "Why did you create a fake e-mail account?"

"So I could get a subscription to a porn site and open an online dating account without your knowledge."

"How much of our money was spent on your addiction?"

"About $1,000."

My jaw drops open. I think back to the number of times I had to go to my mom and borrow money, just to keep my kids fed. We wouldn't even have a house if it weren't for Daniel's parents. Yet he spent a thousand dollars we definitely don't have to fuel his cravings. I feel like I'm going to be sick, but I continue to force out my questions. "Did you ever have sex, in any form, with any of the women you met online?"

"No."

"Did you ever go on a date with anyone other than me?"

"No. I only chatted with them and it was only for a brief time."

"Then how did you meet the woman you had sex with in California?" My voice cracks. This doesn't feel real. This can't be real. This is not my life.

"Some buddies from work and I went to a bar one night and got a little drunk. I don't even know her name."

I suck in sharply. A one-night stand. I don't even know what's worse—a long-term affair or sex with a total stranger. "Did you use protection?" I can't believe I'm asking questions like this.

"Yes. And when I got home and realized what I had done, I had a physical. I do not have any STDs or anything."

I breathe a sigh of relief. "Is that when we started having problems? I know the last year has been one of the hardest in our marriage. Is this why?"

Daniel nods, burying his face in his hands. "Yes. I was so consumed with guilt, I began pulling back from you and the kids. I wanted to tell you so many times, but I was too scared. Then I twisted it in my mind, to protect myself, and blamed you for the affair. I thought if it were your fault, I would be justified in my actions. Going through the program and therapy has reminded me that nothing I did was because of you. Everything I did was my own choice and because of my addiction."

For the first time, Daniel looks into my face and looks me straight in the eyes. "None of this has anything to do with you. You have been my best friend for almost twenty years and you don't deserve any of this. I'm so sorry I hurt you." Daniel slides off his chair and falls to his knees in front of me.

"I'm done now." I look at Ryan as I stand, with support from the chair, and step over Daniel. I walk from the room. My legs are shaking, but I'm determined to at least make it out to my car.

"Sarah, wait," I hear Daniel call after me.

"Let her go," Ryan says. "She needs time and space now."

I move toward the elevator and make my way downstairs. Everything around me seems still and quiet. I feel like my body is moving in slow motion as I make my way down the elevator, out the front doors, and toward my minivan. I fumble with the keys, trying to cram one into the tiny hole. My trembling fingers can't make it fit. I realize I have a keyless entry and push the unlock button. I slide the back door closed behind me and lock the car. Then I crawl along the floor of the van, collapsing onto the back bench. I begin to shiver, my body shaking violently. I reach under the bench and fumble around until my fingers grasp soft fabric. I pull out a blanket and wrap my body tightly, pulling the cover over my head. I shake and scream and cry until my body finally gives out and I fall asleep.

Chapter Fourteen

I wake up with the worst headache I've ever felt in my life. My head throbs so intensely I can barely open my eyes. Through the slits I can see it's starting to get dark outside. I stumble off the bench and fall to the floor of the van. I'm confused until I remember why I'm in the minivan. I think back over all I learned in the disclosure. The bile in the back of my throat finally wins out. I have to yank the sliding door open and barely make it in time to puke in the parking lot. I wipe my mouth and look around. All the cars are gone. Everyone has left for the day.

I slide the back door closed and climb into the front seat. I rest my head on the steering wheel. I can hear my phone buzzing in my purse. I look down through squinted eyes and fumble around in a side pocket until I locate the buzzing. I grip the edges of my phone and pull it out just as the vibrating stops. Two missed calls from Melissa and one from Breanna. I'm not ready. I close the phone and drop it back into the depths of my open handbag.

I take a few deep breaths and back out of the parking stall. Through labored breaths and squinted eyes, I drive down the road. A car turns in front of me and I slam on my breaks, barely stopping in time. I look up. The light is red. When it changes back to green, I crawl forward. I'm not sure where I'm headed until I pull in front of my mom's house. I climb out and stumble up the front walk. I lean on the doorbell and close my eyes.

She opens the door. "Well, Sarah, this is a nice surp—" She stops mid-sentence. One look at my pale face and puffy eyes and she practically carries me into her house. "Oh my word, Sarah, what's the matter? What happened?"

I lean back on her fluffy, crocheted couch pillows and close my eyes. I have to put a hand up to block the bright lights in her living room. "Mom, can I get some water and Ibuprofen, please?"

"Sarah, you look white as a sheet. When was the last time you ate something? I can't give you Ibuprofen on an empty stomach. It will just make you sicker."

"I honestly don't remember, Mom."

"All right, you just rest right here. I'll be right back."

I don't remember falling asleep, but I must have because my mom begins shaking me. "Sarah, here, sit up and eat this." She puts a peanut butter and homemade jelly sandwich in my hand and sets a tall glass of milk on the coffee table in front of me. She points to the sandwich. "Eat." I may be thirty-five years old, but when my mom uses that tone, I don't argue. My mouth feels like cotton and still tastes like dried vomit. The sandwich is delicious and I eat it way too quickly. After I drink half the glass of milk, my mom opens my hand and places three little white pills in my palm. "Take those," she demands in her don't-argue tone. I place the pills on my tongue and swallow them down, emptying the glass of milk.

She sits next to me on the couch, wraps an arm around me, and in a much gentler voice says, "Now talk."

I start at the beginning and leave nothing out. My mom listens to every word without interruption or criticism, which is exactly what I need right now. I struggle when I get to the part about Daniel cheating on me. I can't get the words out past my lips. My breathing grows ragged. I'm gasping for air. My head spins and I can feel the sandwich like a rock, churning in my stomach. My mom runs to the kitchen and comes back with a small paper bag. "Here, breathe." She hands the bag to me and I place it around my mouth, scrunching the top of the bag in a fist. I breathe in and out as best I can. Soon, my heart begins to slow and my breathing returns to normal.

My mom sits back down beside me and pulls my head onto her lap. She runs her fingers through my hair while I cry on her couch and finish my story. I can't look her in the face. I stare at her coffee table and the little knick-knacks she uses to decorate it. After a long silence, my mom says, "Daniel is a good man. He reminds me a lot of your dad. He always has. I wish you would never have to go through this pain, but I feared you would someday suffer this heartache, too."

I sit up quickly and stare at my mom. "You mean... ?"

"Yes, sweetie, before your dad died, we struggled with this awful addiction for years. We didn't have the resources and information you do now."

My head is swimming. How is it possible that every single person I seem to know has this addiction, but no one told me anything until now? Why are people so afraid of talking about it? I grip my head between my hands. I can feel the throbbing in my temples against my fingertips.

"Do you remember when you and I lived with Aunt Bea for a few weeks?" my mom asks.

"I remember we went to visit her. You told me that it was a special mommy daughter vacation."

"I lied. I found out about your dad's affair and left for two weeks so he could break it off and clean his porn stash out of our house. I gave him an ultimatum before we left. I told him to have everything gone, or to be gone himself. I honestly didn't know what we would return home to."

I'm speechless. My dad was an addict? "How did I never know? You guys always seemed so in love." I choke on the last word.

"There are lots of evils in this world, my dear. No one is perfect. Your daddy and I had our fair share of struggles, and he spent plenty of nights on the couch.

But we loved each other very much. A perfect marriage is just two imperfect people who refuse to give up on each other." I recognize the quote as one my parents kept beside their bed while I was growing up.

Mom strokes my hair, brushing the loose strands behind an ear. "Don't think less of your dad. He was weak but in the end, his addiction made him stronger. And he loved you more than anything in the world. He spent the rest of his life trying to make up for his mistakes. I'm sure Daniel will do the same."

I pull out of my mom's grasp and stand up. "But I don't know if I want him to! I don't think I'm strong enough. I can't live the rest of my life looking into the eyes of a man who betrayed me." I grab my purse off my mom's floor and head for her front door.

"Sarah, please come talk to me."

"No, mom, I'm done listening to confessions for tonight!" I slam her door and rush for my car, even though she isn't following me. I start the engine and drive. My phone begins buzzing like crazy, so I fish for it with my right hand while holding the steering wheel with my left. It's pitch black outside now. I'm sure it's well past my kids' bedtime. But I can't do it. I can't go look into their beautiful, innocent eyes and tuck them into bed as if my whole world isn't crumbling around me. I can't pretend tonight. I don't have the strength. And I know they're in good hands with Melissa. I pull over and look at my phone. Six missed calls from Melissa, three from Breanna, and over a dozen text messages. I turn my phone off and chuck it back into my purse. I pull back onto the road and flip a U-turn. I know where I'm headed now.

I pull into the empty parking lot and find a spot in the back, so my car won't be seen from the road. The large trees overhead make the night seem even blacker. A few street lamps line the paved path, offering an eerie, faint glow. A low mist hangs just above the ground as I climb from my car and traipse through the wet grass. There is a bitter chill in the air, biting at my nose and fingertips, yet I can barely feel the cold through the heat raging inside me.

I pull a flashlight out of the glove compartment, thankful we stuck it in there for emergencies. I flip it on, shining the beam across the grounds to light the path ahead. I haven't been here in years. I wonder if I'll be able to find it. I crunch through the few leaves that have started to fall already. I shine the flashlight back and forth over the ground, looking for the right spot. I recognize a bench and turn toward it. A large grey stone juts up in my path. I step around it and shine my light on a flat marble stone in the ground.

Edward Paul Gregson

I drop onto the damp grass and set my flashlight on the headstone. "Hi, Dad." I sigh and stare at the date engraved beneath his name. I pick some of the taller grass growing around his grave and rip it into miniscule pieces. "I wish you were here, Dad. I'm struggling right now and I really could use your advice. You and I could always talk so much easier than I can with Mom. We never had any secrets."

I grab a fistful of grass and chuck it. "Only I found out tonight that you lied to me my entire life! You had a disgusting, dirty habit and you kept it hidden from me! I can't even believe you cheated on Mom. She didn't deserve that! All she did was love you, and you betrayed her!" I stand up and stomp all over my dad's grave, yelling at both the ground and the sky. The bottom hems of my pant legs are completely soaked. The cold begins to seep in through my wet shoes and socks. I shiver.

"Why couldn't you just be the dad I thought you were?" I crumple to the ground, my bare arm slamming into his stone. The cold marble bites against my skin. I rest my head on my arm. "Why, Daddy?"

I lay on the cold stone, shivering when an image jumps into my mind.

Daniel's blue eyes are sparkling as he stares into my own. The shock is still written all over my face, causing Daniel to chuckle.

I choke on the word. "Twins?"

Daniel takes my hand in his and kisses it sweetly. "It will be okay," he says. "We can do this together."

"But twins?" My throat feels dry and raspy.

"Just think of it as an adventure. Olivia is old enough to help now. Think of how much she'll love holding one of her little brothers or sisters in her arms. And Danny can bring you diapers and binkies and blankets."

I shake my head and continue to stare up at the big black screen. "There's just no way. I'm not strong enough."

"It's too late for turning back now," the doctor laughs.

I shoot him my fiercest look and the smile drops from his face.

"I'll just give you two a moment," he says, slipping from the room.

Daniel squeezes on the exam table beside me and pulls me into his arms. He tenderly kisses my head. "You are the most amazing mom I've ever witnessed in my entire life. These two little babies will be more loved and cared for than any one baby in the world." Daniel gently pulls my gaze away from the screen, to look into his eyes. "You can do this. We can do this. You are incredible and I love you." He kisses me until my worries melt into a puddle of warmth.

"How are you feeling?" Daniel pokes his head into our bedroom.

My swollen feet are propped up on two large pillows. My protruding belly blocks my view of the door, but I can hear Daniel's voice coming closer. He peeks around our mountainous twins and smiles. "Can I get you anything?"

I look at him and grumble. "I hate this! Bedrest sucks! I'm bored out of my mind, I can't get comfortable, I can't even take care of my own children, and I'm starting to smell." I reach up and touch my greasy, matted hair.

"You smell like radiance to me," he says, bending down and kissing me lightly on the lips. "But if you feel gross, I'd be more than happy to help." Daniel carefully slides one arm under my shoulder blades and hooks my legs with his other. He scoops me into his arms and walks carefully over to the master bathroom.

"I can walk ten feet," I say.

"Nope. Those little girls need to stay in as long as possible. It's your job to take care of them. It's my job to take care of you."

Daniel helps me undress and sets me into the warm bathwater. He begins gently massaging my scalp with shampoo.

I sigh. "Thank you. That feels wonderful." I close my eyes and then almost immediately open them again. "Where are the kids?" I ask, trying to sit up. The house is too quiet."

"Your mom took them to the park for a little while, to give you a break."

"I don't need a break," I say. "They're my kids and my responsibility." My hand slips on the white porcelain when I try to stand.

Daniel catches me and pulls me back down. "She's a grandma. Let her play that role once in a while. I know you're strong, but you also need to take it easy." He pours a cup of warm water over my head, filling the tub with suds.

"What about you? Shouldn't you be in school or doing homework?"

Daniel bites his lip. "Would you just learn to relax?" he teases. "I took the semester off to help take care of you. School is important, but my wife and my family come first."

The pregnancy hormones begin bubbling inside me like a volcano, threatening to burst out through my emotions. "Thank you," I choke out. "Thank you for taking such good care of me."

"Of course, babe. You're my girl. You're the one I chose to take care of forever."

The frigid dew seeps through my pants, piercing my legs and feet. I shift and sit up, tucking my shoes under my body, but remain leaning against my father's tombstone. I see Daniel again, his pleading eyes begging for my help in his darkest hour. I can see the sincerity in his eyes, the humbleness in his voice. I watch as he scoops our girls into his arms. The absolute joy in their eyes when he holds them, and takes them to dinner for a daddy daughter date. I see a crying baby boy, shortly followed by his sleeping figure in Daniel's arms, the dried chocolate smeared around his smiling mouth. Then I see him sneaking into our kitchen early in the morning, and a hot plate of pancakes sitting on the counter. The last image I see are the tears pouring down his face while he admits the affair. He didn't have to do the formal disclosure with me. It was his choice. He asked Ryan if we could. I think of Breanna and Joe. He could have chosen to leave at any time, like Joe did.

I push up on my elbows and kneel in the grass. My memories flash back to when I was a little girl. I don't remember my dad ever missing a soccer game or a single choir performance. Our monthly daddy daughter dates were the highlight of my life. He would always let me choose where we went to dinner, without complaint. Then he'd order a large dessert to share and let me eat most of it, until I felt sick. My mom's words stand out: "He spent the rest of his life trying to make up for his mistakes." I know what she told me is true. My dad was the most loving, attentive husband and father anyone could ask for. Just like Daniel. Daniel made his choice. Now it's my turn.

Praying has become more natural now. I fold my arms across my chest and bow my head. "Father in heaven, my heart is breaking. I feel betrayed by both my father and my husband. But I have also seen the good in them. Father, I want to forgive them. I need to forgive them. Please give me the strength to give up this anger and find forgiveness. Please take this bitterness and this burden from me. Help me see the hope in our future. Help me to feel sincere love for my husband again, the way I know you love him, without conditions or restraint. I need your help, Father. I know I can't do it without you. In Jesus name, amen."

The warmth starts in my chest and burns throughout my body, encompassing my fingertips and down to my toes. I stop shivering. I can only feel the fire lit from within. I smile, sincerely smile, and look heavenward. Tears stream down my face, warming my cheeks. I get to my feet and blow a kiss at the headstone below. "I forgive you, Daddy," I whisper. "I love you forever."

"Sarah?" I can hear my name being called, but it can't be real. I look up. "Sarah?" I hear my name again. This time the voice is getting closer. I shine my light ahead and squint into the darkness. "Sarah!" Daniel rushes toward me, stopping short a few feet away. "Everyone has been so worried about you! When you never showed up to pick up the kids, Melissa called me in a panic. She and your mom took the kids home and put them to bed hours ago, but we were all so worried! No one could reach you on your phone. Your mom told us you left her house hours ago."

I stare down at my dad's grave and blink several times. Hours? I've been here for hours? I look back up at Daniel, who continues to talk.

"Breanna is scouring the city with some guy, looking for you in every bar and restaurant she can think of. I'm so sorry, Sarah. I never wanted to hurt you and I never wanted to break us."

I smile. He found me. I rush forward into Daniel's arms. The shock of my movement and the force in which I hit him almost knocks Daniel to the ground. I lean into his chest and breathe. He wraps his strong arms around me and holds me tightly against him.

"Your mom told me about your dad tonight. I'm so sorry, Sarah! That's when I decided to check here. I'm so glad you're safe."

I look up into Daniel's beautiful blue eyes and only see love radiating out of them. "I forgive you," I whisper softly.

Daniel's eyes widen, glistening with moisture. "You do?"

"Yes. I want to go home. Daniel, please take me home. And this time, don't leave me there. Stay."

Daniel lifts my feet off the ground in a tight embrace. I hug him back with equal force. "I love you, Sarah."

"I love you, too."

Chapter Fifteen

I wake up feeling more rested than I have in a very long time. Which is surprising given the late hour we got home last night. I glance at the clock. It's 7:15 a.m., which means we got a little less than four hours of sleep.

A hand reaches out and his warm, strong arm drapes over my body. I stiffen at first. I haven't been held like this in several months. Daniel scoots closer so his body is pressed against my back. "I miss this," he whispers. "I miss just holding you in my arms."

I soften and slowly sink into his embrace. "I missed this too." I'm not ready for anything more than snuggling yet. He may have my forgiveness, but he still has to earn my trust. For now, this is really nice.

Jaxon stumbles into our room, clutching his blankie and a stuffed dog in his arms. "Mommy?" I sit up and reach my arms out for him. He climbs up the edge of our bed and falls into them. "I love you, baby." Jaxon looks over and notices Daniel in our bed.

"Daddy?" His confusion quickly breaks into a smile. "Daddy!"

"Hey, little man," Daniel hugs Jaxon close to him. Daniel then lifts Jaxon above his head, his arms extended, and tickles him. Jaxon squirms and giggles.

The noise draws Olivia to our room. "Mom, you're home! What happened last night? Aunt Melissa was totally freaking out."

I pull Olivia down onto the bed bedside me and hug her tight. "I'm so sorry, sweetheart." I look at Daniel, and then back at our oldest. "My meeting went a lot later than I thought it would, and then I wasn't feeling very good. I needed to rest."

"Dad!" Olivia shouts, seeming to notice him for the first time. Daniel lands Jaxon down on the pillows and sits up. Olivia runs around to the other side of the bed and hugs him. "You're here! Does this mean you're all better now?"

"Well, I still have a long ways to go, but I'm well enough to come home now."

Olivia squeals. The twins come running into our room and jump on our bed, joining in the party. "Daddy! Mommy!"

"OOF!" Maddy jumps into Daniel's chest, knees first. I look at him and laugh. "Welcome home."

He smiles back, rubbing his chest. "Gee, thanks."

Danny enters our room. "It's Saturday. Can't I sleep in?"

Daniel and I exchange a glance. "Actually," I say, "your dad and I have some fun activities planned for today. We thought we should spend the whole day together as a family to celebrate Daddy coming home."

Olivia jumps to her feet. "What are we doing?" she asks excitedly.

Addy jumps off the bed. "Where are we going?" She bounces back up.

"It's a surprise!" I say. "Now go get dressed, quick. We have lots of fun to do."

Daniel picks up Jaxon. "I'll go get this little guy dressed if you want to hop in the shower first."

I notice Danny doesn't say anything to his dad, but he leaves our room quickly to get ready, along with his sisters. I smile and make my way to our bathroom.

When I come out dressed and ready to go, I can hear laughter coming from the kitchen downstairs. The sound warms my whole heart. I walk down the stairs and discover Daniel wearing one of my aprons, standing over the griddle flipping pancakes. The apron is far too tight for his broad frame. I giggle at the sight. Daniel looks up and smiles. "What?" he says, posing with his spatula in the air. "Don't you like my cute outfit?"

The kids all burst into laughter again. Daniel continues to pose for us. I pull a plate from the cupboard and hold it out. "Three, please."

Daniel looks at me under raised eyebrows. "Hungry?"

"Starving! Now give me the goods."

Daniel plops three hot pancakes onto my plate and then pats my bottom with the spatula when I turn to walk away. Olivia smiles, Danny rolls his eyes, and the twins giggle again.

After everyone has had their fill, we pack a picnic lunch and pile into the minivan. Daniel helps buckle the kids in and then opens my door for me. I sigh in relief. I hate driving, and I've had to do all of the driving for our family the last three months. I'm excited I get to be a passenger again. I buckle my seatbelt and sit back, a broad smile stretching across my face. Nothing can ruin this day. That's when my phone rings.

"Hello?"

"WHERE HAVE YOU BEEN?" I have to hold the phone away from my ear while Breanna continues to yell at me. "Do you know how worried sick I was about you all night long? Bronson and I combed the city looking for you. I even checked alleyways, afraid I would find your dead body somewhere. You were supposed to call me the minute you got done with your disclosure so we could talk through it. What kind of person promises to call and then disappears all night long? I get a text from Daniel at three freakin' thirty in the morning to tell me he found you and you were safe. That's it! No details or nothin'! All right, missy, spill!"

I slowly move the phone towards my ear again. "Can I talk now?" I ask hesitantly.

Breanna huffs into the phone. "I was so scared something terrible had happened to you," she says more calmly.

"I'm so sorry I scared you. Last night was... rougher than I thought it would be." I glance at

Daniel, who looks back at me. I reach across the seat and he squeezes my hand. "I am home, I am safe, and Daniel is actually home now, too."

"What?"

"A lot happened last night. But right now we are actually in the car, driving to a special family day. So I will call you later tonight with all the details, okay?"

"That's what you told me last night and I spent the evening afraid my best friend was dead!"

"Okay, first of all, stop watching so many crime shows on TV. I will call you tonight. I promise."

Breanna huffs again. "Okay, fine. I love you."

"I love you too, Bre."

I hang up and chuckle. "She's a bit dramatic," I say.

"Okay, but in all fairness, you really did have a lot of people worried."

"I know, I'm sorry."

"Mom?" Olivia's calls from the back. "What happened last night?"

I sigh. Thanks, Bre. "You know what, honey? Let's talk about it later. Right now I just want to go on our adventure and have fun together as a whole family again."

I play I Spy and 20 questions with the kids to keep them entertained while we drive. When Daniel pulls up to the waterfront and drives around in search of a parking place, Olivia squeals. "Are we going on a ferry ride?" she asks.

"We sure are," Daniel says.

The kids all cheer and begin fighting their way out of their seats.

"Wait, please." I turn in my chair. "Leave those buckles on until Dad is parked."

The race is on once Daniel parks the car. All the kids scramble out, except Jaxon who can't do his buckles yet on his own. He wails until I climb out of the car and release him. With Jaxon on my hip and Addy's hand in mine, we walk toward the loading dock. Daniel grabs our picnic lunch and holds Maddy's hand, following right behind us. Olivia and Danny race ahead. We climb on the ferry and the older two insist on going to the top deck.

"All right, but be careful and stay together," I instruct them. Daniel and I take the younger kids to find a seat toward the front. When the engine purrs to life, Jaxon giggles. They love looking over the edge into the blue-green water below as the ferry cuts a path through the waves.

We climb off the ferry onto a beautiful, sandy beach. A red and white striped lighthouse looms overhead. Daniel pulls a Frisbee out of our large tote bag and tosses it to Danny. He runs after it and catches the disc right before it hits the ground.

"Yay!" I cheer him on and Jaxon runs toward his brother. "You did it, Danny!" he yells. He trips in the deep sand, his hands sinking in when he hits the ground. Danny drops the Frisbee and runs over to pick him up. He brushes the sand off Jaxon's hands and clothes. Then he carries his little brother over to the

Frisbee and shows him how to throw it. Jaxon tosses the disc almost straight down at his feet, but we all cheer for him anyway. His two-year-old face lights up and he giggles. "Again!" Danny helps him throw the Frisbee again, this time with a little extra help, and we watch as it sails through the air toward Olivia. She jumps up and clamps it between her hands.

"My turn!" Maddy calls.

Olivia throws to her little sister and soon we are all standing in a big circle, taking turns throwing the Frisbee to each other. Daniel and I stand opposite each other, to make sure the disc can fly far enough to make it to the other side of the circle. I look up at the beautiful sunshine. There is a light breeze in the air, but the weather is unusually warm for fall. I close my eyes and smell the wonderful salty air. I feel like this day is a gift from God.

When the kids get bored with Frisbee, Daniel pulls out a soccer ball and the twins begin chasing him through the sand. Daniel kicks the ball to Olivia, who kicks it to me. I dribble between my feet and then kick it to Danny. Maddy and Addy run from person to person, trying to get the ball from one of us, which quickly turns into a game of Monkey in the Middle.

The girls squeal and scream until they realize they can't get the ball from any of us. Their giggles turn into cries of frustration, effectively ending our game. I pull out a large red picnic blanket and spread it across a flat piece of beach.

"Lunch time!"

Everyone plops onto the blanket in a semi-circle and we begin to enjoy our sandwiches and fruit.

"Daddy, why did you leave?" Maddy asks.

The question causes Daniel to choke on his bite of turkey. I begin coughing and notice Danny puts his sandwich on his lap and looks away.

"Well, sweetie, Daddy got very sick and I needed to stay with your aunt Melissa for a little while so I could get better."

"But you're back forever now?" Maddy asks, her eyes pleading.

"Yes, I'm back forever now," he says, pulling her onto his lap.

Danny shakes his head and then jumps to his feet and begins running across the cool sand toward the lighthouse. I get to my feet and follow him.

"Danny? Danny, wait up!" I chase him until my legs throb and my side hurts. Thankfully he collapses in the sand only a few yards away. I walk over to him, clutching my side, my feet sinking with each step. I fall onto the sand beside him. He sits up and turns away from me, hugging his knees.

"What's going on, Danny?"

"Nothing."

"Danny, please talk to me. I know something is wrong." I gently place my hand on his shoulder, slowly turning him back to me. I wrap my arms around his slender frame and he falls into my lap. I hold him quietly and wait. I feel a hot, wet tear slide down my leg and have to bite my lip to keep my mouth closed.

"How can Dad say that?" Danny whispers so quietly, I have to lean down to hear him.

"Say what?" I whisper back, matching his tone.

"How can he say he'll stay forever? What if he gets sick again? What if you get divorced? What if I don't get good grades like Olivia and he leaves?"

I can feel a lump rising in my throat. "Oh, honey!" I wrap my arms around him tighter and rest my chin on his head. "Is that what's been bothering you lately?"

He slowly nods.

"Danny, your dad loves you very, very much! He didn't want to leave, trust me. But now he is working on getting better. I can't promise he won't get sick again, but he will never, ever leave you. And his leaving had absolutely nothing to do with you. Do you understand me?"

Danny sniffles and wipes his nose with the back of his shirt sleeve. He nods. "Are you guys getting a divorce?"

"No, Danny, we're not. I'm sorry we made you so worried. I promise I will talk to you better in the future about things like this. I keep forgetting how old and mature you're getting. I didn't want to worry you."

Daniel walks over to us and pauses a few feet away. I wave him closer and he sits on Danny's other side. I stand up carefully, leaving the two of them to talk. When I get back to our spot, Olivia is playing Duck-Duck-Goose with the three youngest. I sit in the circle between Jaxon and Addy and wait for my turn.

I hear a low rumble and look up at the sky. Grey clouds are beginning to roll in, and the wind picks up. I glance around to see Danny and Daniel walking back toward us. A few fat drops begin to fall. "Okay, guys, time to go!" I gather all the leftovers and garbage from our lunch and stuff them back into the large tote bag. The wind blows and several wrappers scatter. "Quick!" I yell, pointing. The kids race after the litter, trying to catch them mid-air.

I grip two corners of our picnic blanket and Olivia takes the other two. We almost have it folded when the rain begins. I grab Jaxon in my arms while Daniel swings the heavy bag over his shoulder and we run for the docks. By the time we reach the ferry, every one of us is completely soaked. Daniel's brown hair is matted down against his face, his shirt dripping with water. Olivia, Maddy, and Addy's hair are stringy, their shoes sloshing with each step. All five of the kids are shivering. Looking at each of them, I can't even imagine what I look like and the thought makes me laugh.

"What's so funny?" Danny asks.

"We all look like drowned little puppy dogs."

We glance at each other and laugh. Maddy and Addy begin barking. Daniel finds a bench seat in the center of the boat and guides us to it. We sandwich the four kids between us and huddle close to stay warm. Jaxon curls up on my lap and falls asleep against my shoulder. Daniel stretches his arm behind the kids and I stretch mine towards him, so our fingers brush against each other at the back of the bench. Today was perfect.

Chapter Sixteen

*D*ear Sarah,

I can't even express in words how happy I am to see you've chosen to forgive your husband and work through this tragedy. Right now you are in the honeymoon phase of recovery. Everything feels wonderful again as you and Daniel begin reconnecting. Don't stop your recovery because you feel happy! Recovery is never over. It takes a conscious effort on both parts to keep the addiction dormant. Remember everything you have learned in group and through therapy. You have the strength and the tools now to work together as a team and push through the difficulties that will arise in your future. Everything will not be perfect and easy, but you can make it!

Sincerely, a friend

This is my first e-mail in over a week. I thought after I forgave Daniel, my friend had pulled back and disappeared. I guess not. I wonder how long he/she will continue sending them. I sigh. Recovery is a lifelong battle. Ryan has been telling us this since the beginning, but it seems so final, written down in print right in front of me. Ryan assured us it will become easier as the years pass, but we just can't get lazy about it. I take a deep breath and begin getting ready for the day. I'm not a quitter.

Today is the beginning of fall break. All the kids are still sleeping, so once I'm dressed and ready, I make myself a cup of coffee and sit on the back porch. The air is crisp and cool. The colorful leaves swirl around me with each blow from the breeze. I sit back and take a deep breath, warming my nose before I sip. The breeze picks up, so I pull my sweater more tightly across my chest. I hold the striped mug between my numbing hands and take another sip.

The pattering of little feet against the hardwood brings me back inside. Maddy and Addy are sitting on the couch watching cartoons, a bowl of dry cereal in each of their laps. I peek in the kitchen and notice the barstools pushed up against a high shelf in the pantry. Cereal spilled on the counter where they tried to pour out their own. I smile and pick it up. At least they're getting independent.

Olivia comes down the stairs, yawning. She moans when she sees what show the girls have chosen.

"Why do we only have one TV?" she asks.

"To keep our family safe. One TV is plenty. You can always take turns watching shows if you don't like this one. Or even better, read a book!"

Olivia rolls her eyes at me. I stick out my tongue and cross my eyes in response. She laughs. "Fine," she says, sitting down and pulling the cereal box toward herself. She reaches a hand in and pulls out a sugary handful, leaving a trail of crumbs where I just cleaned up. I hand her a bowl and a washcloth. "Try again."

Jaxon makes an appearance at my side, his arms loaded down with stuffed animals. He drops the pile at my feet and asks for breakfast. Once the kids are all happily munching on cold cereal, I begin dusting the house. The last few months not only took a toll on me, it took a toll on my poor house. I can hardly see my furniture under the thick layer of white dust. I start with the living room, making sure to move in slow motion as I wipe down the TV screen.

"Mom!"

"Move!"

"We can't see!"

I chuckle as I move on to the den. Per my requirements, Daniel's computer is now set up in our sitting room. The room has turned into a small office instead. After our family outing, Daniel and I spent the last week selling or removing a lot of our electronics. Now we are a one TV and one computer family. Both are in high traffic rooms, neither of which has a door. I dust the newly framed family picture that rests on Daniel's desk beside the computer. It was taken by a stranger on the ferry, when we were all dripping wet and laughing. It's my favorite picture from that day. Every time I look at it, I remember it as the day my family started fresh. It's like God gave us a do-over on life.

When I begin dusting the keyboard, my hand accidentally brushes against the mouse. My heartbeat quickens and my breath catches in my throat. I'm overwhelmed with a funny feeling to check the browser history. I close my eyes and shake my head. I don't want to. I feel anxious and slightly dizzy. My stomach is swirling with butterflies. I try to stand and walk away, but I can't shake the feeling. I return to the desk and, with a shaking hand, move the cursor over our internet browser. I glance at the history and immediately have to close it again when I click on the most recent website. The disgusting images that pop up make my heart stop. My eyes burn. My breathing grows short and ragged. My hands begin to shake. Tonight. Daniel and I were going to install the new filters on the router tonight.

I stumble down the hallway and into the bathroom. All that delicious, warm coffee forces its way out of my stomach and into the toilet in streams. I collapse onto the cold tile floor. Sweat runs down my face, my entire body begins to shake.

Daniel and I were gone all last night. We had a therapy appointment with Ryan and then he took me to dinner and a movie afterward. My mom watched the kids. When we got home, we both went to bed. Daniel used to frequently get in trouble after I went to bed and the house was dark and quiet. One of our new rules is we go to bed together every night. I'm a super light sleeper. I know if Daniel had gotten out of bed. I would have woken up. Then this morning I watched him get ready and leave for work. There's no way it was him.

My mouth is forced open again. I throw up everything that was left in my stomach. I continue to heave until my entire stomach and chest ache.

I flush the toilet and fall down again, breathing heavily. My mind is spinning with the new realization. I force myself back up and rinse my mouth in the bathroom sink. I step out of the bathroom and walk slowly back through the living room. Danny is sitting crisscross applesauce on the couch. He smiles at the TV and laughs. I stare at my beautiful nine-year-old boy. How could this have happened? He glances at me and smiles, his eyes shining. "Morning, Mom."

I smile weakly and then race upstairs. I immediately call Daniel at work.

"Hello?"

I try to speak, but my voice can't crack through the emotions. I begin breathing heavily again and fear a panic attack is about to start.

"Sarah?" Daniel's voice sounds panicked. "Sarah, talk to me, what's wrong?"

"I think Danny is looking at porn." Even as the words pass through my lips, I can't believe them.

Daniel is silent. I glance at the screen, wondering if my phone dropped the call. "Daniel?"

"We need to deal with this together. Hold off and we can talk to him together tonight. Okay? Don't panic yet, Sarah, not until we know what happened."

I nod my head, even though he can't see me. In my mind, I see Danny flashing me his smile again. "I'm not sure I can wait until tonight. I won't be able to keep it together all day."

"I'm on my way home. Just hang in there."

"What about work?" I ask.

"Work can wait. We need to take care of this now. I'll tell my boss I'm not feeling good and take a sick day. After what you just told me, I definitely won't be lying."

Daniel and I hang up the phone. I lay back on our bed until I can get myself composed. I call my mom and ask if she can come over to take the younger kids to the park. I don't have to give her much of an explanation before she quickly agrees and says goodbye. I take several deep breaths before I return downstairs and ask the kids to get dressed. I can't look Danny in the face as he brushes past me. The morning moves as if in slow motion. My mom arrives just when I'm about ready to explode. She picks up Jaxon and guides the twins out to our car. I hand her the keys to my minivan.

My mom pats my face as she walks by. "It's going to be okay," she whispers. "You can do this."

I try to smile but her words make me feel more like I want to cry. Daniel walks past my mom as they're leaving. His mouth is drawn down, his face solemn. He takes me by the hand and we go up the stairs to Danny's room. Danny looks up in surprise when we enter.

"Hi, Dad, what are you doing home?"

"Hey, bud, can we talk to you for a minute?" Daniel asks.

Danny shrugs and plops down on his bed. "Sure."

I sit beside him on the edge of the twin mattress. Daniel pulls the desk chair over and sits across from us. We look at each other, unsure where to begin.

"Were you on the computer last night?" Daniel asks.

"Yeah, I was doing my homework. Why?"

"Your mom found a really bad website when she turned on the computer today."

"We're not mad at you, Danny, but this is really serious. Why did you go to a site like that?"

Danny's eyes widen. "I didn't do anything!"

"Danny, we just want to know who showed you that website. Who told you about it?"

"I didn't do it!" Danny says, jutting out his chin. His eyebrows narrow and he folds his arms across his chest.

There's a light tapping on the door. We all turn and watch as Olivia enters. Her face is white, her eyes red and swollen. "It was me," she whispers, hanging her head.

My heart feels like it's been pierced by ice. "You?" my voice cracks.

Olivia nods and then rushes into my arms, sobbing. "I'm so sorry! I didn't know!"

I stroke her hair with my hand while cradling her in my arms. "Oh, Olivia."

"I told you I didn't do anything," Danny mumbles.

Daniel strokes his forehead. "I'm sorry we didn't believe you, Danny. That wasn't very fair of us to assume."

"Can I go now?" he asks.

"No, we need to have a talk about this. All of us." Daniel scoots beside Danny on the bed. The four of us squish together and for a brief moment, I remember when it used to be just the four of us. I can almost imagine the little four- and six-year-olds they used to be.

Olivia's sobbing slows, but she remains face down in my lap, unwilling to look any of us in the eye. I gently lift her head and brush a strand of hair from her face, carefully tucking it behind her ear. "I love you," I tell her, staring straight into her swollen green eyes. "Now we need to know if this is the first time you looked up a website like that."

Olivia nods her head fiercely. "Some friends at school were talking about it and laughing. They said it was really funny and I need to check it out."

"What did you tell you to look up?" Daniel asks. I can see his jaw tensing and I know how badly he wants to go talk to some fifth grade parents.

"Naked kissing." Olivia glances at Danny. They both look down.

"Did you see it, too?" I ask Danny.

He slowly nods. I reach over and rub his back.

"How did you guys feel when you saw those images?" I ask.

"Yucky," Olivia says. "My tummy has been hurting ever since."

I look at Danny. "What about you?"

"I felt… slimy."

"Why didn't either of you tell us about what happened?" Daniel asks.

"We didn't want to get in trouble," Olivia says.

"So you knew it was wrong?"

They both nod.

"I need you both to understand something," Daniel says. "Do you know what addiction is?"

"Yeah," Olivia says.

"I… think so," Danny replies, looking confused.

"Addiction is a horrible, awful thing. It takes away your ability to make choices. Do you remember when Mom and I talked to you about drugs and alcohol and cigarettes?"

They both nod.

"Why did we tell you to stay away from those things?"

"Because they're bad for us," Olivia says.

"That's right, they're really bad for you. And if you drink alcohol too much or smoke a whole bunch, you can become addicted. That means every day, instead of going to school with your friends, all you care about is smoking, or taking drugs. You don't get to choose to have fun anymore because the addiction takes over your brain."

"Can't you just stop?" Danny asks.

Daniel shakes his head. "When you're addicted, you can't stop by yourself anymore. You have to go to special doctors and they have to help you. But it's really,

really hard and it hurts a lot. When you're a grown-up, addiction can also make you lose your job and your house and your whole family. It's like a really terrible disease." Daniel sighs deeply and presses on. "When I had to move out and go live with Aunt Melissa for a few months, it was because I have an addiction."

Danny's head snaps up. Olivia's eyes widen.

"When I was younger, some friends showed me pornography, just like those pictures you two were looking at. But instead of stopping, I kept looking. As I got older, I looked at bad pictures more and more. Pretty soon, I couldn't really think about anything else. Remember how awful I was last year?"

"You yelled a lot," Olivia whispers.

"And you were gone a lot," Danny adds.

Daniel flinches. "You're right. That was the addiction taking over my whole brain. So that's why I had to leave for a while. I didn't want to lose my family. You guys are the best things in my life and I love you more than anything. I went to lots of special doctors and Aunt Melissa helped, too."

"Are you all better now?" Olivia asks.

Daniel leans across the bed and pulls our big eleven-year-old onto his lap. He kisses the top of her head. "I'm working every day to be better so I can deserve you guys."

She wraps her arms around his neck and kisses his cheek. "I'm glad you're getting better."

Danny looks down and his chin begins to quiver. I wrap my arms around him. "Danny, what's wrong, sweetie?"

"Do I have an addiction now, too?"

I tighten my hold around him. "No, sweetie. But it's very important that next time you see something that makes you feel funny, or you think might be bad, come tell Dad and me. I promise we won't be mad. We just need to know so we can help you."

"And just like if a friend offers you a cigarette or some drugs, if someone tries to show you pictures like that again, just tell them no thanks and walk away."

"Why are those pictures bad?" Danny asks.

I look at Daniel and wait. I hope he has an answer. I don't know how to explain this to our children.

Daniel glances at me. "Well, as humans, we're supposed to be attracted to each other, right?"

The kids both slowly nod, their eyebrows crinkle.

"Let me try this again. You guys are old enough, you can tell what's real and what's pretend, right?"

"Yeah."

"When you were little, you were scared of monsters. Your brain didn't understand they weren't real. But now you know that monsters are just pretend."

They both nod more enthusiastically.

"Well, Mommy and Daddy love each other. We're attracted to each other. We are both real. But pornography is like the monsters. It's pretend feelings of attraction. And if you look at these pretend pictures for too long, your brain can't have real relationships anymore. Does that make sense?"

Danny stares up at Daniel, his eyes thoughtful. "So pornography tricks our brains?"

"That's right."

The garage door downstairs opens and soon the house is filled with boisterous laughter and echoing feet on the hardwood. "Sounds like the littles are back," I say.

"We can talk about this more later. Are you guys okay?" Daniel asks. "Do you have any more questions?"

"How do we make the yucky feeling go away?" Olivia asks, rubbing her stomach.

I gently pull the kids off the bed and we kneel together. "Let's say a prayer," I suggest.

Chapter Seventeen

D*ear Sarah,*
Don't be afraid to reach out and help others. Your own recovery becomes stronger when you share your hope and knowledge with people who find themselves in your shoes. Just as many have helped you on this journey, go and do the same.
Sincerely, a friend

I smile at the e-mail. I know exactly what this person is getting at. Where this e-mail might have offended me before, I know they speak the truth and are only trying to help me succeed. I haven't been to my support group in two weeks. We've had a dance recital and a soccer game the last two Wednesday nights. But I also know I could have attended a different group on another night. I need to go tonight, I know that. When I first went to group, I hated all the happy, positive people. Now I'm one of them! I definitely need to go help spread some hope. I don't think I would have come this far so fast without the support of those incredible ladies.

I stand over the sink, opening cans of tomato sauce while hamburger browns on the stove. My mom walks into the kitchen. "What are they doing out there?"

I glance out the back window, over the sink. "Oh, Daniel is helping the kids build a treehouse." I wipe my wet hands on a paper towel and add sauce to the hot pan. Without asking, my mom pulls spaghetti noodles out of the pantry and breaks them before adding the pasta to the boiling pot of water on the stove.

"Thanks," I say, stirring the sauce.

"First the new bookshelves, now a treehouse? Wow! Someone is sure working hard."

"I know. He also does the dishes every night after dinner and has been giving me foot rubs at the end of the day." I peek out the window again and smile at Daniel.

"Sounds like you should kick him out more often."

"Mom!"

She grins wickedly and winks. "What? Too soon?"

I shake my head and finish preparing dinner. "Thanks for your help," I say, as my mom begins tossing the salad. "I invited you over for dinner to eat it, not to cook it."

She shrugs. "I'm not just going to stand here and watch you do it all."

"Are you nervous for tonight?" I ask.

"I'm not sure what to expect. I wish they had support groups when I was your age, I'll tell you that. I'm just not sure what to say."

"You don't have to say anything. You can just sit and listen if you'd like. I just thought you'd appreciate the opportunity to go to one and see what they're like."

When my mom smiles, the corners of her eyes crinkle. "I do appreciate the invite. And Breanna doesn't care that I'm joining you?"

"No, of course not." I open the pantry door to throw away a greasy napkin and notice a pile of food in the garbage can. Upon closer examination, I find the underwear catalog that came in the mail yesterday, torn and covered in what appears to be several cans of cream of chicken soup. I meant to shred the magazine when I first saw it and then got pulled away by kids and forgot it until now. My heart swells with pride. Looks like he found his own way to rid the house of temptation.

I close the pantry door and begin laying food out on the table. With my mom's help, we finish making dinner quickly. It takes a lot of coaxing for the kids to abandon their treehouse for another day to come in and eat. Daniel follows them inside, wiping the sweat from his brow. He kisses me lightly on the lips as he passes through the kitchen to wash his hands. He's been gaining the weight back and replacing it with muscle. His face is also filling out again and doesn't look so gaunt. He glows with happiness. I'm so happy to have my husband back.

I walk into group tonight without hesitation. Breanna walks beside me, talking animatedly with her hands while she gives all the details from her latest date. We make it to the refreshment table before noticing my mom isn't with us. We both turn and see her standing in the open doorway, unmoving. I motion for her to come in and join us. She looks around at all the women, who almost completely fill the chairs in the circle. Her eyes are wide with fear. It's going to be a large group tonight. I wave to my mom again. She shakes her head and looks back toward the exit. I walk across the circle towards her.

"It's okay, Mom. They don't bite."

She glares at me before stepping into the room. "I just didn't realize there would be so many," she whispers.

"It's an epidemic, Mom."

Breanna manages to convince a few ladies to scoot down so she can secure three seats together. I guide my mom over to her and we sit. My mom rests on the very edge of her seat, as if she might jump up and run away at any moment.

"This is just so embarrassing," she whispers, looking around again. "Maybe I shouldn't have come."

"Mom, there's nothing to be embarrassed about. You didn't do anything wrong. There will be no judgment from any person in this room when we're all going through the same thing."

She sighs and sits back in her seat, but remains stiff. I try not to smile. I know I felt the same thing at first too. The meeting begins just as a beautiful woman walks into the room. Her eyes are sparkling, her smile inviting. "Sorry I'm late," she whispers as she finds the last remaining seat across the circle. I can't help but stare. She seems so familiar to me. Her long brown hair is curled to perfection and bounces beautifully against her slender shoulders. Her smoky eyes, an effect I've never been able to master, pop against her soft pink sweater. My eyes are drawn to this woman while the discussion circles around us. I try to look away, but my gaze continues to find her. As sharing reaches her side of the room, my own eyes widen when she begins speaking and realization strikes. A lot can happen in two weeks of absence.

"Hi, my name is Hailey."

"Hi, Hailey."

"I just wanted to thank you ladies for being here to support me. My first week here was... a difficult one." She looks across the circle at me and smiles. I smile back, tears pricking the corners of my eyes.

"I didn't plan on coming back. I was too ashamed of what my husband has done. He is... very far gone into this addiction." She looks down and swipes at a tear as it rolls down her cheek. "But during the last two weeks I couldn't get your words out of my head. I've had a lot of dark days. Days I couldn't even get out of bed. You witnessed one of those days last time I was here, I believe. A friend told me about these groups and found one online for me. I rolled out of bed and came, mostly because I couldn't stand being alone with myself and my thoughts anymore." Hailey pauses when her emotions take over. "Sorry," she whispers while trying to regain composure. She blows out a breath. "I even wanted to take my own life." Her voice shakes.

There is an audible gasp in the room, but a couple of women nod.

"My husband is not a kind man. I sometimes wonder if he ever was, or if it's always been an act. He lies, he manipulates, and he puts on a fantastic façade so everyone around us thinks he's amazing. I used to think he was amazing. He has been physically and emotionally abusive for most of our marriage." She wipes away another stray tear and shifts from one foot to the other. "But, it was the words I heard when I came to this meeting the first time that have gotten me on the right path. Words like self-care, and addiction, and therapy. I can happily report that I have been taking time every single day for myself. I don't get dressed up and do my makeup to show off for others anymore, or because my husband wants me to. I don't look nice for anyone but me. I'm eating healthier and exercising, and I've started seeing a therapist twice a week. And you know what? I'm not ashamed anymore! My husband always convinced me therapy is for weaklings. I know now just how wrong he was. Therapy is for the brave! It's for those people strong enough to admit they need help."

The women in the room begin to applaud. Her cheeks flush pink and she waves the applause down.

"I don't want anyone here to judge me, but I left my husband a week ago and I have decided to file for divorce. He doesn't see himself as having a problem. He puts the blame for everything wrong in our relationship on me. He has made me feel so small and so insignificant for too long. I'm finally beginning to feel free. I know I have a very long way to go. I've been co-dependent on him for nearly seven years. But actually packing my bag and walking out, no matter how terrifying it was, made me feel strong. It made me feel human again." She looks up and offers a tiny smile. Her eyes dart around the room anxiously as she pats her leg. "So, I guess that's all. I just wanted to say thank you for making me feel loved and accepted." She looks at me again before sitting back down.

The sharing continues around the circle, moving quickly. As soon as Breanna sits down, I stand next. "Hi, my name is Sarah."

"Hi, Sarah."

"I know we aren't allowed to cross-talk, but Hailey, no one in this circle will ever judge you for choosing divorce. Some of us can work through this addiction with our spouses, but only if our spouses want to work through it. Others can't." I glance down at Breanna. "You can't force anyone into recovery. You can only choose what is best for your circumstances and that choice can't be made by anyone but you. And especially if you aren't safe in a relationship, mentally or physically, then it might not be a relationship worth fighting for."

The women clap their hands again and several nod their agreement. Hailey smiles at me, her eyes shining.

"Daniel and I are doing well. I missed group the last two weeks due to conflicting activities with my children, and I felt the difference. I was a little more anxious these last couple weeks. I found myself wanting to share with you ladies the events of my day. Tonight, for the first time, Daniel is at home watching the kids while I'm here. I didn't have to bring them to my sister-in-law's house and I didn't have to call my Mom to babysit. They are with their dad, who is home." I smile broadly.

"We had a scare a couple weeks ago when we discovered two of my children had looked up pornography online. But Daniel and I talked to them, and we did it together. He admitted to them how this has been a struggle for him and how this addiction almost destroyed our marriage. I can't believe how honest he was with them. It was beautiful to witness."

I sit down and to my surprise, my mom stands next. She introduces herself and shares her brief history with my father. "My husband passed away four years ago. I thought I had worked through all of this while he was still alive. But after listening to you ladies talk tonight, I've realized there is still some hurt there. I didn't realize how much of myself I had allowed to shut down with his death. I will definitely be coming back next week. Thank you." I reach over and squeeze my mom's hand. We exchange a smile and turn to listen to the next woman.

After group, I walk across the circle and approach Hailey. Before I can say a word, she throws her arms around my neck. "Thank you." I return her hug and we hold each other for a moment.

"I almost didn't recognize you," I say, stepping back.

She laughs. "I know. Not one of my best days."

"We've all had our first time here."

"I'm so glad you came tonight," Hailey says. "I prayed you would, and here you are! I just wanted to say thank you for everything."

"Why does your thank you feel like it comes with a goodbye attached to it?"

Hailey glances down. When she looks up again, she's biting her lip and her eyes look moist. "I'm moving back to Oregon. I'm going home to stay with my parents for a little while. I need help with my son while I go through recovery and figure out my next steps. I just wanted to tell you thank you before I left."

I hug Hailey again. I pull out my phone. "Can I at least get your phone number before you leave?"

She smiles. "Sure."

"Please text me anytime," I say. "I hope you'll find a support group out there."

"Definitely."

"But if you ever need someone else to talk to, please call or text me."

"Thanks, Sarah. Good luck. I'm rooting for you and your family."

"Thanks. Bye, Hailey."

"Bye."

My heart aches as I watch her walk away. I hope she stays in contact.

Breanna and my mom are standing by the door waiting for me. I approach them and they both move in for a group hug. "She'll be okay," Breanna says.

I look after her. "I sure hope so."

"Let's go get some ice cream," my mom suggests. "My treat."

"You go," Breanna says. "Bronson is picking me up for dessert."

We walk outside together. I see a handsome man leaning against the building. He smiles broadly when he sees us. His crooked teeth make him that much more charming. Breanna squeals next to me and I can tell by her quickening pace that she wants to run to him. He meets us and leans down to kiss Breanna.

"Bronson, this is my best friend in the entire world, Sarah Dunkin."

"Nice to meet you, Bronson," I say, holding out my hand.

"And this is her mom, or my second mom for most of my life, Eleanor."

"Pleasure."

My mom shakes his hand.

Bronson takes Breanna by the arm and leads her to his car. They wave a final goodbye as Mom and I climb into her car.

"Did you say something about ice cream?" I ask, buckling my seatbelt.

"Yes, let's go. After all that emotional stuff, I could really use some chocolate." She pulls out of the parking lot and begins to drive.

"Mom, have you been sending me e-mails?" I ask. It occurred to me tonight that I haven't asked her yet.

My mom glances over at me. Her wrinkled brow says enough. "I don't do e-mail, honey. You know me. If I'm going to talk to someone, I want it to be in person or over the phone."

"I know," I say. "I'm just out of ideas about who could be sending them."

"What type of e-mails are they?"

"Just little messages from someone anonymous. They started the morning after I found out about Daniel's addiction."

"What types of messages?"

"Words of encouragement and wisdom about this addiction and recovery. Whoever this person is, they've been guiding me since day one."

"Well, are the e-mails helpful?"

"I didn't think they were at first, but yes. They are extremely helpful."

"It sounds to me like they're a blessing, honey. Why would you want to question a blessing?"

Chapter Eighteen

I t's Christmas morning. The house is completely quiet while I sit by the golden glow of the Christmas tree. The sun will be up any minute now, which means the kids will be, too. For the moment, I'm enjoying the silence of the morning, the warmth of the fireplace, and the beauty of the tree. There is something so peaceful about Christmas lights. I finish tying the bow on Daniel's present and place it under the tree, pushing it behind several boxes. I want to be sure it's the last gift opened.

I tiptoe into the kitchen and remove the towel from the rising cinnamon rolls for our traditional Christmas breakfast. I stayed up late last night rolling them out and now they look perfect. I place the first pan in the oven and begin mixing the frosting. My nose itches so I reach up to rub it with the back of my hand and end up smearing powdered sugar across my face. Four months ago, I wasn't sure if I would still even be married by Christmas. Now I'm happier in my marriage than I've ever been.

Daniel relapsed two months ago. On Halloween night, actually. All the skanky costumes triggered him and then he had a lot of stress at work to deal with. He was working late that night. I had just gotten the last of Danny's green monster paint washed from his face and the kids tucked into bed when Daniel arrived home. He looked broken. He immediately fell to his knees and told me what happened. We held each other and cried.

I sent him upstairs to pack a bag and he left for Melissa's house. It was so much easier to explain this time, with Olivia and Danny knowing the truth. We spent the next day apart. It was an extremely rough week. We spent some extra time in Ryan's office and I became an emotional puddle in group. I spent much of the week crying on my knees, but this time, we made it through together. Daniel is more determined than ever to remain sober.

As rough as that week was, I learned a lot. We had all the right steps in place, which helped the healing go so much faster this time. My relationship with Daniel is stronger than it's ever been. As awful and hard as some days have been, I wouldn't go back and change a single moment. Without the trials, we wouldn't be as solid as we are today. I look across the kitchen and into the living room. The golden lights from the tree seem to be shining with hope. I think back to what Ryan said about *Kintsugi*. I'm definitely not going to hide our cracks with glue or sweep them under the rug. Our cracks show how strong and beautiful we have become. Like the tree, they glow with hope for the future.

I pull the first pan of cinnamon rolls out of the oven when I can hear giggling making its way down the stairs. I glance up in time to see the twins heading into the living room. Their eyes widen at the modest pile of gifts. They look at each other and then begin jumping up and down.

"Santa came!"

"Santa came!"

I kneel and beckon them to me. Wrapping them both in a tight hug I whisper, "Merry Christmas."

"Merry Christmas, Mommy!"

"Now, why don't you guys go wake up Daddy and everyone else."

They scream and race back up the stairs yelling, "It's morning time! Santa came!"

Daniel comes down the stairs with Jaxon in his arms. Olivia and Danny follow closely behind him. The sun is just peaking over the trees outside, illuminating the sky with a soft pink. Jaxon practically leaps out of Daniel's arms to get down. The kids all sit around the couch and the floor, comparing their stocking goodies with each other.

Daniel comes into the kitchen and wraps his arms around me from behind. He kisses my neck. "Merry Christmas," he says quietly in my ear.

I turn and wrap my arms around his neck. "Merry Christmas," I say back. He reaches out and wipes the powder off my nose with the edge of his finger. I crinkle my nose at him. It tickles. Then he snitches a scrap of dough. "Gross," I say, whipping him with the kitchen towel. He grins and jumps out of the way.

"Mom, Dad, come on! Let's get started!" Danny yells.

"Hold your horses. Grandma isn't here yet," I call back.

The oven beeps. Daniel grabs a hot pad and pulls out the baking sheet. Warm cinnamon and brown sugar waft up to my nose. I pull out the cream cheese frosting and begin spreading it generously over the tops of the warm cinnamon rolls. The frosting melts into them, seeping into every crack.

The doorbell rings and all five kids go screaming for the door. Daniel and I both look up. Poor Jaxon trips over his own feet and splats onto the hardwood. My mom walks in and scoops him up amid the bouncing and excited chatter. The kids show Grandma every treasure from their stockings. "Why haven't you opened any presents yet?" she asks.

Five heads snap in my direction. "Mom said we had to wait for you," Olivia explains.

"Well, maybe we should start with these ones then." My mom sets down a large tote bag. Brightly colored packages spill out. Addy lunges for one with her name on it, squealing with anticipation.

"Wait for us," I say, grabbing my phone off the counter and settling on the couch to snap pictures. Daniel sits beside me.

"And... go!" he says.

The kids begin tearing into the presents Grandma brought. Maddy jumps up and down and hugs her. Then she runs over to me, showing off her new toy. It doesn't take long for the bottom of the tree to look bare again. Only one small box remains. I reach under the tree and pull it out. I hand it to Daniel. "Merry Christmas," I say.

He looks at me and down at the football tickets he holds in his hand. "You already got me an amazing gift," he says. "I don't remember the last time I actually went to a game."

"This one was last minute," I say.

He pulls off the bow, lifts the lid, and peeks inside. His lip twitches. Then he starts off grinning and ends in a broad smile. "Seriously?"

I nod and laugh. "Seriously."

He pulls out the positive pregnancy test and holds it up for everyone to see. "I'm going to be a Daddy again!"

Danny grumbles, but the three girls all start cheering and talking about baby names. Jaxon is busy with a sucker he found in his stocking and has no idea what's going on.

Daniel puts the test back in the box and sets it down. He wraps me in his big arms, pulling me off my feet. "I'm so happy," he whispers.

I chuckle. "Good, 'cause there's no going back now."

My mom hugs me. "Congratulations. Six. Wow!" Her mouth hangs open.

"I know. But I'm super excited about it!"

We shuffle into the kitchen, prodding the kids to leave their toys momentarily and join us. I dish a cinnamon roll onto each plate while Daniel pours milk and juice into cups.

The doorbell rings just as we're starting to eat. Daniel looks to me. I shrug. We both get up and answer the door. Breanna and Bronson are standing on the porch. Breanna's hand is shimmering brightly in the sunlight. I step forward, grabbing her left hand and pull it to my face. "Oh my gosh!" I scream and hold her hand toward Daniel.

Breanna laughs. "I told you she'd notice right away."

Bronson shakes his head and smiles. "Fine, I owe you ten bucks."

I scream again and pull Breanna into the house. "How? When?"

"This morning. It was waiting for me under the tree." Her smile is so big, it lights up her entire face.

Daniel invites Bronson into the house. "Congratulations!" he says, shaking hands with him and slapping him on the back. "It's about time you made an honest woman out of her."

Breanna slaps Daniel in the stomach and they both laugh. He then pulls her into a tight hug. "Congratulations," he says. "We love you so much and we're so happy for you."

"Thank you," she says, smiling up at him.

"Do you want to see what I got for Christmas?" he asks.

"Of course."

Daniel hurries from the room and comes back with his small box.

"And here I thought you were going to show her your football tickets," I tease.

Daniel hands the box to Breanna. She opens the lid and screams. "No way!"

I laugh and the hugging starts all over again.

Madison and Olivia come in to see what the commotion is all about. "Aunt Breanna!" Maddy exclaims, leaping into her arms.

"Hey, kiddo!" Breanna holds Maddy on her hip and turns to Olivia. "Do you want to see my Christmas present?" she asks, holding out her hand.

Olivia looks at the ring with wide eyes. "Wow! It's beautiful! When are you getting married?"

"We haven't gotten to setting a date yet."

"We didn't even get to eat breakfast," Bronson says. "As soon as she said yes, Breanna was on her feet telling me we had to hurry over here."

"I feel your pain," Daniel says. "Well, we have plenty of Sarah's famous homemade cinnamon rolls. Come into the kitchen and eat with us."

Bronson's stomach growls loudly. "I think I may just take you up on that."

Daniel leads the way into the kitchen. Breanna links her arm through mine and we follow behind the men.

After breakfast we move into the living room and visit while the kids enjoy their new toys. Breanna and I exchange details about our amazing Christmas gifts. My mom goes back and forth between playing with the kids and joining in on our conversation.

"I hope I'm as good a mom as you are someday," Breanna says.

"You'll be amazing," I say. I Point to my brood, who are strewn about the floor and running in and out of the room. "You've had plenty of practice."

"I'm going straight from single woman to wife and step-mom. It's a little scary."

"You'll be amazing," I say again.

"Actually, Ashley is five. Maybe I should bring her over to play with the twins one day."

"That would be great! The girls would love it."

"Then you can teach me all your fabulous mom tricks."

I laugh. "Do you want to know a secret?" I ask. Breanna leans closer. "I make up the tricks as I go along."

She laughs. "Great."

My phone dings loudly. I glance at the screen. "Would you excuse me for just one minute?"

"Of course." Breanna slides closer to Bronson when I stand up, resting her head on his shoulder.

I make my way upstairs and sit on the edge of the bed. I open my inbox and read the new message.

Dear Sarah,

The time has come for my e-mails to end. I am so proud of you and the journey you have taken. Even though I will no longer be actively present, I will never be far away. You know how to reach me now. Talk to me anytime. I'm always here. I love you more than words can express. Every time you look into one of your precious children's eyes and feel the warmth in your heart, know that is how much I love you. My son hurt you deeply, but you chose to love him unconditionally in return and now he is becoming the man I always knew he could be. Thank you for loving him. A very precious little girl will be joining your family soon. Cherish her as you do each of your other children. She will make your family complete. I love you, Sarah. Remember how much I love you when times are hard. Get on your knees and talk to me whenever you need guidance and peace. I will always be by your side.

Sincerely, your loving Heavenly Father

I stare at my little screen until my eyes burn and I'm forced to blink. What? This can't be real. I can feel tingles begin in my lower back and crawl all the way up my spine until they reach the base of my neck. I shiver. I feel warm and happy. I subconsciously reach down and place a hand on my belly. Another girl? I close my eyes and smile. Only time will tell. I close the e-mail and get to my feet. Whether it's real or not, I'm not going to question it. I'm just going to be grateful for the blessings this friend has brought.

I walk down the stairs and find it has grown very quiet. "Where is everyone?"

"The kids wanted to have a picnic lunch in the treehouse, so everyone went outside," Daniel calls from the kitchen.

I find him making the last of the sandwiches, a large stack piled on a plate beside him. He hands me the plate, grabbing a pitcher of water and a couple bags of chips.

"Shall we?" he asks with a bright smile.

I stare into his shining azure eyes. I see all of our children in those eyes. I see the hope in our future shining back at me. I stand up on my toes and kiss him on the lips. "I love you."

"I love you, too."

He balances the water and chips in one hand while he pulls open the back door. The sun is shining brightly overhead. There's a crisp chill in the air, but it's unusually warm outside. The kids are chasing each other and laughing. Daniel sets the food on the patio table and takes off after them, crunching across the grass. He growls and chases them, tossing Jaxon high into the air when he is caught. My mom and Breanna are hunched together looking at wedding dresses online with Bronson by their side. I smile and step outside to join my family.

Epilogue

I t's been one year. One year since I ran downstairs to ask my husband a simple question and caught him with another woman. One year since my life changed. And guess what? I feel good. In that year I have truly found myself. I discovered an inner strength I never knew I had. I made friendships I will cherish forever. And most importantly, I found God. I still don't know if the e-mails were really from him, but it doesn't matter. I choose to believe they were. I never told anyone else about that final message, but I read it over and over again whenever life gets hard.

For our sixteenth anniversary, Daniel gave me a package. The return address was listed as Japan. Inside the box was the most beautiful jade bowl I have ever seen. The bowl is completely covered with cracks, like it had once been shattered. Shining through the cracks, especially when I hold the bowl up to the light, is the glint of gold. The bowl rests in the center of our mantle as a constant reminder. I know our journey is far from over. Daniel attends his 12-step meeting regularly, and we still check in with Ryan once a month. We have good days and bad, just like everyone else. Every day when I see that bowl shining in the sunlight, I'm reminded what we're fighting for.

Hope is two months old now. She is so full of life and joy, I thank God every day for sending her to us. I pray regularly now and I can feel his strength helping me through each day. The last year has been filled with trials, but it has also been filled with triumphs. We have spent one year making our marriage stronger. One year reconnecting. One year of heartache, and one year of joy. One year of tears, and one year of laughter. I refuse to view this day with dread and sadness. Instead it is the one year anniversary of when we reclaimed our marriage.

A Note from the Author:

I spoke to many women about their experiences with an addict husband before writing this book. Everyone's journey through this addiction will be different. I tried to cover a variety of situations, but for the sake of the story, I could not dwell on every possible circumstance. Many will struggle financially, many will struggle with family and friends not being supportive, and most will need support groups and therapy.

Although I believe marriages are worth fighting for, I also know not everyone will be as lucky as Daniel and Sarah are. If both partners are not fully committed to recovery, addiction can feel like an impossible battle. Recovery and forgiveness are not an easy road to travel, but I do know that they are possible. Everyone's journey will be different. Some will achieve peace and forgiveness quickly, while others will take years to rebuild trust and overcome feelings of despair. By working together, and through faith and prayer, the Lord has made it possible to overcome all obstacles.

That being said, abuse in any form whether it be physical, emotional, or sexual should never be tolerated. If you find yourself in an abusive situation or relationship, please seek help!

For more information about pornography addictions, check out Fight the New Drug online. It's one of my favorite sites concerning this topic. Here are some great resources for support groups:

General Christian:

    http://www.celebraterecovery.com

LDS:

    http://addictionrecovery.lds.org

    http://www.owningourstories.blogspot.com

Non-religious:

    http://www.lifestarnetwork.com

    https://www.freedomeveryday.org

    http://sanon.org

Acknowledgments:

First and foremost I want to thank my husband. He has been amazingly supportive through this entire journey. He has encouraged me to share our experiences, so others don't have to suffer as we did.

I would also like to thank my incredible team of beta readers: Rachel Jacobson, Ashlee Stratton, Kristie Hall, Angie McFarland, Katie Daimaru, Ricci Howell, Sara Galyon, Candice Toone, and Theresa Young. Without their feedback and input, this book would not exist. Thanks to Ryan and Tammy, who are both rock star therapists! And for all my "sisters" in recovery, thank you for sharing your stories with me!

Finally I'd like to thank my awesome editor Juli Caldwell for always making my manuscripts shine. She is a grammar goddess! And Steve Novak for my beautiful, brilliant cover.

If you enjoyed Shattered Hearts, enjoy this sneak peek of My Name is Bryan:

CHAPTER ONE

"Hardships often prepare ordinary people for an
extraordinary destiny."
-C.S. Lewis

June 1979

"Cliff jumping. You in?" Bryan's smile widened as he watched his best friend's eyes light up.

"Absolutely! When?" Greg asked.

Bryan threw his large duffel bag into the opening under the bus. "I don't remember. I think my dad said it's toward the end of the trip. But apparently we get to conquer some pretty big rapids first."

"Sweet! This trip totally beats what we did last year."

"Yeah, no kidding."

Bryan and Greg stepped away from the bus, wandering across the parking lot to settle under a large oak tree.

"Hey, man, you ready?" Another lanky teenage boy came up to the pair.

"Yeah, my dad was telling me about some cliffs we can jump off during the rafting trip." Bryan could hardly contain his excitement.

"Oh yeah? How high?"

"Not sure," Bryan said, looking around as some other guys approached. "But it sounds awesome."

"What sounds awesome?" one of them asked.

"Cliff jumping," Greg chimed in.

"Seriously? Sweet!"

"Are the leaders going to let us?"

"Yeah, Duane is the one who told my dad about them," Bryan said.

"Hey, looks like we're loading now." Greg pointed at the line of teenagers snaking their way through the parking lot and onto the bus.

Bryan and his friends were the last to get in line.

"Oh, man, that means we're probably sitting up front."

"Loser seats. Right behind the…" Bryan trailed off as they climbed the three steps and found the last two empty rows were directly behind the chaperones, just as he had feared. "Parents," he sighed.

Carol Jean turned around in her seat and flashed her son a huge smile. Bryan tried to return the grin, but it came across as more of a grimace. It was bad enough his parents were on the trip, but now he had to sit by them?

"Oh, Bryan," Carol Jean laughed. She rolled her eyes and turned to her husband, Glenn. "Have you ever seen a more sullen teenager?" she asked.

Glenn turned in his seat and smiled. "Well, he is stuck with all us old fogies. Poor kid can't catch a break. First his boss doesn't want him to come, then he has to travel on his last youth conference trip with both his parents and his sister. Maybe we should start planning his pity party now."

"Okay, thank you," Bryan waved his parents off and turned to Greg.

"Your boss didn't want you to come?" Greg asked, putting on his black aviators and leaning back in his seat. "How come?"

"Summer is the busiest season for pouring concrete, as I'm sure you can imagine," Bryan explained. "My boss couldn't find a replacement so he didn't want me to come." Bryan shrugged. "I was able to talk him into it eventually though."

Greg nodded.

Bryan lay his head back against the soft, grey headrest and closed his eyes. He wasn't tired enough to sleep, but after working hard labor outside every day, it felt nice to just sit and relax with his eyes closed. His thoughts traveled to Jana and he wondered what she was doing at that moment.

As if reading his thoughts, Greg asked, "So how are things going with Jana?"

Bryan opened his eyes and smiled. "Really great! She's amazing and lots of fun."

"So what're your plans? You gonna keep pouring concrete?"

"For now. At least until I can get a job at a garage somewhere."

"Still no college?" Carol Jean asked, trying to hide the disappointment in her voice. She had been eavesdropping from the row in front of them.

"What would I do with college? If I'm going to be a mechanic, the best schooling I can get is in a garage."

"Have you found a garage to take you on as an intern yet?" Glenn asked, trying to turn around in his seat.

"No. I thought it would be better to start applying after this trip. I didn't want to get on somewhere only to tell them I needed a week off."

Glenn nodded his head in agreement. Bryan watched as his dad quickly put his focus back on the driver and the road. His dad had a map in his head and could get anywhere without a problem. He always preferred the scenic route to reaching his destination quickly. Bryan knew it drove him crazy to just sit back and watch as the driver sped past several attractive pullouts. His dad constantly said, "Life is about the journey," before turning down a dusty little side road. But they always ended up right where they needed to be. Bryan smiled as he watched Glenn's lip twitch. He knew it was killing him not to say anything.

Bryan looked down the long row of seats toward the back of the bus, catching his sister's eye. He smiled, but Becky returned to her conversation without acknowledging him. The game was on. Bryan stared, unblinking at the side of Becky's face. His eyes bore into her cheek until it started to turn pink. His eyes narrowed, but still he didn't blink. Becky's mouth twitched at the corners, until she finally broke into a smile. Bryan laughed and turned around in his chair. He had won.

The drive was peaceful, especially compared to family vacations. With four younger sisters, road trips were anything but quiet. There was always fighting over seats or music or screaming at each other to stop touching.

"If both your parents are here, who has your other sisters?" Greg asked.

"Brenda is at a junior rangers camp, and both Glenda and Jenny are staying with a cousin."

"So this must be a nice week off for you, huh, Mrs. C?" Greg asked, leaning forward.

"I'm not sure I'd call rafting through rapids a relaxing week off, but I'm sure we'll have fun."

Several hours later, the bus jostled Bryan awake as they drove over loose gravel, nearing the San Juan River. He hadn't even realized he'd fallen asleep. Once they reached the river and everyone climbed off the bus, they split into smaller groups of ten or so to a raft, and each raft had a chaperone in charge. Duane walked to the front of the group and welcomed them enthusiastically.

"How's everyone doing this morning?" he asked.

"Fabulous, marvelous, and wonderful!" Glenn's response was louder than any of the kids in the group. Several of them turned toward him and smiled. His enthusiasm increased the excitement around them.

Once everyone was quiet again, Duane gave a small lesson on rowing and had the kids all practice smooth, strong strokes together. Once food and supplies were safely loaded, the kids climbed aboard the big yellow rafts and pushed off.

They spent the first two days on the water for a good portion of the day. They pulled off occasionally to eat or explore but spent most of their time working together to row through the brownish green water. They had little time for floating, as the water moved quickly over the large rapids. When they did get moments of calm, the kids got in water fights with the other rafts or jumped in the water to swim and cool off. They had to travel so many miles each day to ensure they'd make it to the next camp site and that the trip would end on time.

Having already turned eighteen, Bryan was one of the oldest kids in the group. He was even in charge of his own raft since there weren't enough adults to go around. He took this charge seriously and watched over his group as he guided them down the smooth river.

On day three, some of his group began to get restless so Bryan devised a plan. They slowed down and waited for Becky's raft to come into view, and then they pulled up alongside it to ambush her and her friends. Several boys jumped aboard, grabbing the screaming girls and throwing them into the water. The girls squealed and tried to get away, but the ambush worked in the end. They not only emptied their opponent's raft, but they were saved from boredom as well. Becky grabbed onto the side of her brother's raft, gasping, and asked Bryan for help. He grabbed her by the lifejacket to pull her aboard, when two other girls popped up from the water and grabbed Bryan, yanking him in. The cold water rushed into his face, burning his nose and eyes. He sputtered and coughed, and then broke his head through the waves, chuckling.

On the last night of the trip, as their raft neared Slickhorn Canyon, Bryan and his friends began talking excitedly about the anticipated cliffs.

"Did Duane say how tall the cliffs are?"

"No. You wanna take bets?"

"Twenty feet."

"Fifty feet."

"One hundred feet!"

Bryan and his friends laughed as two of them jumped into the waist-high water to help pull their raft ashore. Bryan slowly got to his feet and wiped the sweat from his brow. Leaping from the raft and pulling it the rest of the way up the bank, he held the yellow beast steady so his passengers could climb out. Duane appeared at their sides, a glint in his eye as he whispered, "You boys ready?"

They nodded enthusiastically. "Let's do it!"

They hoisted the raft further up the bank. Dinner was underway and several groups of teenagers relaxed around the bank where they had made camp. Excited at the aspect of exploring the canyon and finding the cliffs to jump from, Bryan definitely wasn't ready to be done for the day. A stream flowed into the canyon, forming several smaller ponds. Duane led the way, following this stream past the surrounding area.

"I'll catch up to you guys in a minute," Bryan called. Duane nodded. The boys hooted in excitement as they followed closely behind him, making their way up the steep, red rocks. Bryan had to get his raft secure for the night before he could go. Since he was in charge, it was his duty every night to make sure the raft was tied down and their supplies were safe. Once everything was carefully placed in the shade of some nearby trees, Bryan ran to join the others.

He began hiking in the direction the other guys had gone. He hiked nearly a mile and was about to turn back when he saw them jumping off a ledge that overlooked the water. The crimson cliff stood before him like a towering giant, with arms stretched up toward heaven. A smile spread across his face and he lunged at the overhang; David was ready to take on the mighty Goliath. Bryan could hear laughter growing closer as he climbed higher and higher. His long legs made the ascent easy, and as he grabbed the last dusty ledge, he heaved himself up and over the top. Spending the last couple months working hard outdoors had seriously increased Bryan's muscle mass, so he was able to climb up to the rocky ledge with relative ease. As he watched the other jumpers, some hit the water with pencil-straight legs while others bent their knees, looking as though they were sitting mid-air. A couple of the guys started doing flips off the cliff edge into the water. It seems inevitable that when a large group of guys get together, they try to outdo one another. Bryan watched another buddy flip off the ledge and land feet first in the water below, and then jump up out of the ripples and shake the water from his hair, laughing as he made his way back to the shore to try it again.

Bryan didn't want to do a flip. That just seemed stupid. It's harder to control the way you land, and he was nervous about clearing enough space to keep his head from hitting rocks. He couldn't really just jump either. After the flippers, that would make him look like a pansy. Bryan spent the majority of his life living near a pool, and he spent a large number of weekends on a lake with his family's boat. He was a seasoned swimmer. He had no doubt in his mind that he could show up these boys.

Bryan stepped closer to the edge and looked down, waiting for the others to clear out of his way. With perfectly straight arms raised above his head, he bent his knees slightly for momentum and jumped. A huge smile spread across his face as he sailed through the air, the wind caressing his cheeks as the water neared. Bryan knew he had done a perfect swan dive. He only wished he could have seen how beautiful it must have been to the onlookers. His fingertips touched the cool liquid first, his body forming a flawless straight line behind them. But something was wrong. He was sailing through the water, and the river floor was coming too fast. His hands hit the sand hard. His elbows buckled. Bryan's head smashed into the bottom and with a loud POP, he knew his life would be changed forever.

About the Author

Stacy Lynn Carroll has always loved telling stories. She started out at Utah State University where she pursued a degree in English, learned how to western swing, and watched as many of her fellow students became 'True Aggies'. She then finished her BA at the University of Utah where she got an emphasis in creative writing. After college she worked as an administrative assistant, where she continued to write stories for the amusement of her co-workers. When her first daughter was born, and with the encouragement of a fortune cookie, she quit her job and became a full-time mommy and writer. She and her husband have soon-to-be four children, two Corgis, and a fish named Don.

If you enjoyed this book, Stacy would love and appreciate your reviews on Amazon and Goodreads! She also loves to make new friends! Follow her on Facebook:
https://www.facebook.com/authorstacylynncarroll
Twitter: @StacyLCarroll
Google+: google.com/+StacyLynnCarroll
Or visit her website: www.stacylynncarroll.com